CORONA!

Spock controlled his writhing and opened his eyes . . . "I need help," he said.

Mason backed away, hands clutching her throat.

"I am about to be controlled by Corona," Spock said. "I only have a few minutes of resistance left. I can feel it in my mind. I can hear its thoughts . . . It does not respect us. We are here only for its use . . . And it is about to destroy . . . everything!" His eyes widened.

He's afraid, Mason realized. *He's seen something and it terrifies him!*

Look for STAR TREK Fiction from Pocket Books

CORONA

GREG BEAR

A STAR TREK®
NOVEL

POCKET BOOKS

New York   London   Toronto   Sydney   Tokyo   Singapore

An *Original* Publication of POCKET BOOKS

POCKET BOOKS, a division of Simon & Schuster Inc. 1230 Avenue of the Americas, New York, NY 10020

This book is published by Pocket Books, a division of Simon & Schuster Inc., under exclusive license from Paramount Pictures.

ISBN: 0-671-70798-1

First Pocket Books printing April 1984

15 14 13 12 11 10 9 8 7 6

POCKET and colophon are registered trademarks of Simon & Schuster Inc.

Printed in the U.S.A.

For the Saloon

Acknowledgments

My wife, Astrid, and friends Karen Schnaubelt Turner and Kelly Turner were particularly helpful. Always useful for reference and authority was Bjo Trimble's and Dorothy Jones Heydt's *Star Trek Concordance*, which, incidentally, I helped illustrate in its original publication. Does that mean I'm a trekkie?

You bet.

Alan Brennert has always been helpful, especially when we bearded the producers of *Star Trek*'s abortive second TV series in their dens during story conferences. The idea for *Corona* arose during one such session.

The glaring errors—if any remain—are my own. More subtle differences from the canon are probably matters of interpretation.

Prologue

From horizon to horizon, the sky was filled with a dark purple glow, broken by wisps of milky white and luminous green. T'Prylla felt the crunch of ages-old pebbles beneath her boots, the only sound besides that of her breathing and the space-suit's instrumentation. She had left the station to be by herself for a while, and to watch the rise of the new suns, suns barely a year old.

Station One sat on a planetoid on the outer edges of the Black Box Nebula. The station's crew consisted of T'Prylla, her husband Grake, their two children and two research assistants, Anauk and T'Kosa. In reserve—that is, in the cold storage of suspended animation, to save limited resources—were thirty volunteers, whose expertise ranged from astrophysics to space medicine. T'Prylla herself had once been the most renowned physicist on Vulcan, quite a rarity for her youthful sixty years; but she had run afoul of the Vulcan Science Academy by using unorthodox methods of logical analysis—methods which had brought charges of heresy—and

7

had imposed this kind of self-exile on herself and her family to avoid an even more painful confrontation.

Ultimately, then, she was the one to blame for all that had happened. Discoveries had been made—but not in time to save the thirty in cold-storage, who were as good as dead. She had learned more about Ybakra radiation than any previous scholar—but at what a cost! And she had learned other things she might never be able to tell.

Forty-eight hours earlier, Grake had broadcast the normal-space message they had prepared together. They had deliberately concealed their action from the children. Day by day, the children grew stronger, more willful, directed by a force neither she nor Grake understood; the power the children had over their parents and the station crew was disturbing, to say the least. Had she been human, she might have been near panic.

But there was nothing more they could do. In ten years, the message would reach a Federation buoy far beyond the nebula's outpouring of radiation. The buoy would re-broadcast Grake's words and the science report by the faster medium of sub-space radio. Shortly thereafter, perhaps . . .

But it was too much to hope for. She thought briefly of her distant relative, Spock, a science officer aboard a Federation starship. What would Spock do in a situation like this? She had never had the chance to know Spock well. Despite his human ancestry, he had always been held up to her as an example of what a Vulcan could be, could achieve.

The glow on the horizon brightened. The asteroid was turning inexorably toward the source of their new knowledge, the source of their difficulties—the infant stars.

One by one they appeared, huge oblate reddish blobs of light, their edges diffuse and irregular. They were triplets, collapsed from the nebular dust and gases. Gravity had drawn them into mutual orbits, their own growing mass finally cooking off the fusion of hydrogen deep within the stellar envelopes.

The final stages of their birth—the final collapse into true protostars—had taken less than a month, catching the researchers by surprise. Theory had predicted a much longer period; the discovery of huge sub-spacial mass anomalies in the region of the triple stars had come late, and the intensity of Ybakra radiation had not been foreseen. The resulting interference completely ruled out sub-space communications and all but the most concentrated tight-beam radio signals.

"Mother."

T'Prylla turned as quickly as her suit and the low gravity allowed, facing her son, Radak. He was five years old, too young even for the most basic ritual of Vulcan maturity, *ka nifoor*. His expression was peaceful, contented.

"Mother, we know what Father has done."

He motioned for her to follow, and they returned to Black Box Nebula Station One. There would be no further messages.

And no answers, for at least ten years.

Chapter One

Rowena Mason stood transfixed at the window of the personnel transport. She had spent her entire life on the small, yellow-orange planet Yalbo, more known for its spacedock facilities and mining colonies than its natural beauty. Yet now Yalbo, rotating slowly below, was the most beautiful thing she had ever seen. Banks of dusty yellow clouds drifted over the tan and pink Erling Mineral Massif, casting umber shadows across the rills and valleys where her family had labored for three generations. She had never been off-world before, and pictures could not compare with reality.

The personnel transport rolled to face the huge orbiting spacedock, a spider-web-delicate framework of thin cylindrical supports laced together by lateral beams. Huge banks of work-lights were being switched off and spacedock work crews were withdrawing from the U.S.S. *Enterprise*. Mason had researched the *Enterprise* thoroughly after receiving her assignment: the first Constitution-class ship to be equipped with warp drive, on a continuing mission of research and exploration, she was easily the most famous ship in human history.

The quarterdeck of the *Enterprise* seemed to be the only peaceful location on the ship. Officers and crew had already boarded, but stores were still being loaded through the shuttle bay, and preparations were being made for casting off. Rowena Mason stepped off the transport, uncertain, as she walked through the passageway, exactly at what moment she boarded the *Enterprise*.

She was greeted by the Officer of the Deck in Spacedock, a shiny-faced junior lieutenant who, to Mason's relief, was quite human. Starfleet tended to group humanoid oxygen breathers together as crews to avoid expensive ship refitting; non-humanoid types were grouped in various other categories, aboard ships appropriate to their needs. She could not have met, say, a Medusan (she had had nightmares about them as a child), but she was none too sure what she would do when she encountered a Vulcan or Andorran, both reputedly stationed aboard the *Enterprise*. She was glad for a brief reprieve.

She presented her credentials to the OD, who smiled with formal courtesy and passed them through the security device mounted on one side of his podium. "Permission to come aboard?" she asked, unsure of the procedure.

"Permission granted, Mister Mason. Welcome to the *Enterprise*."

That was another thing she'd have to get used to. By calling her "mister," they were extending her a courtesy usually reserved for officers, both male and female.

"Thank you. I'd like my arrival announced to the Federation News Service as soon as possible. And when do I meet the quartermaster?"

"Uh . . . quartermaster? I'm sorry. You must mean Army usage. There is no 'quartermaster' aboard the *Enterprise*. All quarters are allotted by

11

the ship's computer. Your escort will meet you in a few minutes. You're a bit late."

"I know," Mason said. Only six hours before, she had been happily at work on her history of twenty-second century approaches to quantum electrodynamics, her major at the very small Yalbo University of Humanities. She had managed a fairly stiff curriculum despite her work as an FNS reporter. Mason's parents had disapproved of her academic pursuits, preferring that she immediately join her father in the Union Rare Earths Company as a filial apprentice; her decision to continue at the university had resulted in their cutting off all support. She had gone to work as a stringer for the Federation News Service to keep off the despised Student's Dole, and had gradually worked her way up to a staff position, one of only two in Yalbo's FNS Bureau. The other was held by her boss, a crusty ex-demolisher and closet philosopher named Evanric.

Yalbo supplemented its mining income (and kept its chronically idled mining engineers employed) by serving the Federation as a repair and outfitting station. It was no small story when the *Enterprise* was ordered to put into spacedock around Yalbo for new equipment installations. Mason had covered what aspects of the story she could from planetside. When FNS had asked Evanric to release her for an off-planet assignment, she could have refused, but she had been sitting around, calm and happy, for entirely too long . . . and she was, after all, a reporter. Reporters were supposed to be in the thick of things, not puttering on academic projects in the middle of nowhere. If FNS thought her small-planet articles were good enough to merit such an assignment—and if she happened to be the only reporter in the vicinity other than Evanric, who adjudged himself too old and set in his ways—who was she to refuse?

"There may be some confusion at first, Mister

Mason," the OD said. "We've just spent twenty days undergoing repairs and refit. New installations."

"That's why I'm here," she said.

"To catch us while we're vulnerable?"

Ah, the military mind resenting the intrusion of the press, she thought. "No. To report on the new monitors, observe the reaction of the crew. How the *Enterprise* behaves." She smiled.

The junior lieutenant returned her smile. Such discipline, she thought sarcastically. He didn't exhibit a trace of masculine interest in this new addition to the ship's female population. Correct and polite in every particular—except, of course, for that brief probe of her intentions.

"Mister Mason?" a woman asked.

It took her a second to recognize her own name. She wondered if she would always assume someone was asking for her father. She turned and saw a dismayingly beautiful woman in a red regulation uniform standing in the quarterdeck elevator. "I'm Lieutenant Uhura," she said, stepping forward and offering her hand. "Communications officer. Starfleet thought since we'd be working together off and on, we might as well share quarters."

Mason blinked. No wonder the OD hadn't shown any interest in her. Were all Starfleet women so depressingly, exotically gorgeous?

"Lieutenant Uhura is your escort, Mister Mason," the OD explained.

"Yes, I understand, thank you." She shook the communications officer's hand and followed her into the elevator. "My luggage—"

"It's coming through the shuttle bay," the OD said behind them. "It's all taken care of."

"It better be," she said, half under her breath. "There are two FNS mobile recorders, and if they're damaged it'll take me four years to pay for them."

As the elevator door closed, Uhura looked Mason over quickly. Her smile seemed quite genuine,

13

something of a contrast with the OD. "You're going to do a story on the *Enterprise*'s new monitors?"

"Partly. I'm also interested in the new medical equipment."

"Looks like we'll have quite a shakedown ahead of us. If we ever get to the shakedown . . . Starfleet keeps us very busy, you know. Most of our training and shakedown cruises have turned into the real thing. I don't see any reason this time should be different."

"I'm not sure I'm ready for a real adventure," Mason admitted. She could look forward to a nice, safe bit of investigative reporting—but life among mining engineers had taught her that adventure was a euphemism for serious injury or death. "If an emergency comes up, will I be put off at an outpost or starbase?"

"Not on your life. The captain will make sure you're with us every step of the way. If Starfleet wants monitors, and the Federation wants press coverage, they'll have both, and he won't blink an eye or complain once . . . or let them off the hook. You'll see. You could write a whole book just about Captain Kirk."

"You seem to admire him."

"Seem? Honey, he's the *captain*. I don't think there's a man or woman on board who wouldn't follow him down the mouth of a naked singularity."

"And how does he feel about the press?"

"I don't think the question's ever come up. At any rate, *I'm* happy to see you. They've upped my quarters allowance and lowered my mess bill, just to show you around, duty permitting. And I've already worked my way up to the best quarters in junior officers' country. Plenty of room for two. Privacy, even."

"Sounds like a luxury cruise."

Uhura shook her head. "Like I said, Mister Mason—"

"Rowena, please."

14

"Rowena. Like I said, I don't think there'll be much time for luxury."

"Ship's quarters, junior officers' sector," the elevator announced. The doors opened with a *wheep*, revealing a stark white and gray corridor with impressively massive bulkheads outlined in red.

"Welcome home, honey," Uhura said, leading the way.

Chapter Two

"Jim, I swear, if I'd wanted to be a lawyer, I'd have gone to Tharsis University and transferred to Starfleet Internal Affairs." Dr. Leonard McCoy pulled all the homey lines of his face into an exaggerated scowl and shook his head. "Ten thousand new rules and regulations."

"It's just a watchdog, Bones."

"I feel more out of my element every year. First they change my tools, then they tell me the computers can run surgery better—and what's that make me, an electrician?—and now they say that a starship medical center has—" he assumed an air of great dignity and self-importance, "has a 'potential for social disruption.'" His eyes protruded slightly as he stared at Captain James T. Kirk, demanding a response.

Kirk's look of sudden humor and mildness was almost equally exaggerated. "It's all part of the new Federation monitors. They just don't want you to become a god, Bones."

McCoy's explosion of breath showed he didn't appreciate his friend's humor.

Kirk walked between the banks of equipment in the rebuilt medical center. Starfleet had shipped the Transporter Emergency Recovery unit to Yalbo's spacedock months before the *Enterprise* had finished her last mission—along with the command and medical monitors. "If I'm going to have a Federation-programmed watchdog system breathing down my neck, why should you get off—with our chief engineer's pardon—Scot free?" He stopped, turned to look at McCoy, and gestured at a man-sized cylindrical vat filled with transparent green fluid. "If it's any comfort to you, I find it all a bit much, myself. This . . . this . . ." He shook his head. "In my day, the TEREC would have been called a miracle. But now, if there's a transporter accident, you—you, Bones! Good ol' country doctor—you can direct the last memory bank impression of a transporter passenger into this machine, and a virtually exact duplicate can be recreated. No more transporter deaths, Bones."

"It could be a damned nightmare."

"Yes, indeed. A mad doctor could ransack the memory banks for impressions of passengers, combine them, run them through the TEREC . . . create entirely new people. So we have the medical monitors, and the new regs."

Kirk knew all too well that McCoy was simply blowing off steam. McCoy's pretended distaste for new medical equipment, new techniques for saving lives and preventing misery, was a front, behind which the doctor carefully adjusted all his past medical experience. Kirk played along with the theatrics, but not without having some fun of his own. "Why, without the new regs, you could make your own nurse, Bones. She would be—"

"Sexist," McCoy accused.

"She," Kirk reiterated, "would be about five feet

ten, an excellent physical specimen, brainy and as obedient as a Tau Cetian fawnbird. And when you were done creating her, you'd promptly marry her, and Starfleet would lose its best ship's doctor."

McCoy seemed about to either laugh, become apoplectic or prepare a lengthy defense when the com chimed and Kirk answered. "Quarterdeck to Captain Kirk. Wellman, Captain. Mister Mason is aboard and all her equipment is stowed."

"Why should that concern you, Jim?" McCoy asked, puzzled.

"Thank you, Mister Wellman," Kirk replied to the OD. "You may secure the quarterdeck and resume your space duties." Kirk drew up the right corner of his mouth ruefully. "We have a member of the fourth estate aboard the *Enterprise*, Bones. We are now under surveillance. Watch your language."

"I'm a Southern gallant from way back," McCoy said.

"She's here to see how we react to the monitors, and I understand she wants to do a story on the new sickbay."

"I have nothing to hide," McCoy said, making a magnanimous sweep with his arm. "Except my doubts."

Kirk toggled the intercom switch. "Lieutenant Uhura's quarters," he instructed the unit. "Leave a message. I request the company of Mister Mason . . . no, make that Miss Mason . . . at the captain's table in the officer's mess this evening for dinner. Extend my compliments."

"Quite the gallant yourself, eh, Jim?" McCoy's grin was almost indetectable.

Chapter Three

The *Enterprise*'s crew facilities were clean, comfortable and slightly worn-looking. Past refittings had concentrated on updating equipment and not redecoration.

Lieutenant Uhura's quarters were a notable exception. They were richly, tastefully decorated with hanging fabrics, a non-regulation assortment of pillow-couches and a chair made especially for the extremely sensitive skin of a Deltan—a chair which was sheer heaven for a human. Sculptures ranging in size from a few centimeters to one meter betrayed Uhura's particular obsession, collecting surrealistic and totemistic modern African ebony carvings.

Mason had settled into Uhura's cabin, looked over the diagrams of the ship Uhura brought up on the room's video display, and received the invitation to the captain's table for dinner. There was little time for anything beyond a quick cleanup.

She greatly appreciated the *Enterprise*'s lavatory facilities. They were perhaps ten years more modern than the general run of bathrooms on Yalbo. She

19

wondered how she'd adjust when they returned her to her home. Perhaps . . . and it was just an idle fantasy . . . perhaps this story would be her ticket to better things.

In the officer's mess, she seated herself at the end of the six-place table, where her name was illuminated in ghostly green beside a setting of ship's stainless and a dimpled plastic plate. It wasn't her style to be early, but she had miscalculated the time it would take her to get to the mess. The elevator—also called a "turbolift," she reminded herself—was very fast.

A few minutes later, officers began to come in. From the pictures Uhura had shown her, she recognized the chief engineer, Scott; the chief helmsman, Sulu; the science and first officer, Spock, and the computer officer in charge of the monitors, Veblen. Seated at another table was an Andorran lieutenant, an expert in navigation, like many of his race. The sight of the Andorran and Spock made her stiffen. There were no aliens on Yalbo, only humans—no indigenous life forms, no visitors or advisors or tourists. She had heard stories from her mother and father about aliens carrying strange diseases, preaching strange and perverse philosophies . . . and while she had rejected much of that during her years in school, enough of it had taken to make her uneasy.

There was, first and foremost, Spock's severe handsomeness and his ears. The color of his skin—a warm, light brownish-green—was disconcerting, but not that unusual. She had met humans from other star systems who hadn't looked much different. But she knew. He was half human . . . half Vulcan. And he was seating himself at the same table, in the seat next to Kirk's on the right, directly across from her. While she examined Spock, Scott sat on her left. To Spock's right was a stocky, boyish-looking lieutenant who introduced himself as Jan Veblen.

Next came Dr. Leonard McCoy. McCoy sat at the end opposite Kirk's place, greeting her with a nod and a warm smile. "Welcome aboard," he said. She took to McCoy right away. He reminded her of her father—or rather, of her father on one of his better days. "I hope you're finding everything to your satisfaction."

"I haven't been aboard very long," she said. "It seems fine."

"The food here is quite tasty," McCoy said. "But I wouldn't order whatever Mr. Spock is having." Spock surveyed Mason coolly.

"Dr. McCoy is well aware I take my meals in my quarters. I am here purely for the social aspects of dinner with one's fellow officers."

"Spock is a very social fellow," McCoy added. Spock raised one eyebrow but said nothing more until the arrival of the captain. As Kirk approached the table, everyone in the mess rose. She slowly followed suit. Kirk approached her and held out his hand. "On behalf of the officers and crew, may I extend a formal welcome aboard the *Enterprise?*"

"My pleasure," she said. Kirk was roguishly handsome, perhaps forty-five or slightly older. He seemed fit and looked perhaps eight years younger. He took a seat at the head of the table. The rest of the officers resumed their seats and a mechanical steward began carrying a column of stacked plates from table to table, starting with theirs. "Tonight," McCoy said, "we have the boon of the ship's best New Orleans chicken gumbo. One of my favorites, if I must choose."

"We regret not having the time to visit your planet or allow any sort of liberty," Kirk said. "We've been quite pressed. Our last mission was a difficult one, and we'd have enjoyed the time off."

"Well, there's really not that much on Yalbo," she said. She so hated that name. As a girl, she had called it Yellow, which at least had the virtue of being descriptive. "For tourists or visitors, I mean."

"Just very fine engineers and excellent drydock facilities," Scott said enthusiastically.

"Yes, well, we're just about the only spacedock for a hundred parsecs. I imagine that's why you were instructed to come here."

Kirk nodded. "How long have you been a reporter?"

"Three years. On staff, that is. I'm also finishing my doctorate at Yalbo University of the Humanities." That sounds so provincial, she thought.

"The only FNS reporter on Yalbo?" McCoy ventured.

"There's my boss," she said. "His name's Evanric. He used to be . . ." She hesitated. "He's a very good reporter. He used to be a demolisher . . . ran a B and B machine . . . uh, Boring and Blasting. He's my taskmaster here. I mean, on Yalbo. He taught me most of what I know."

"We plan to spend a week on shakedown," Kirk said. "Though I imagine Mr. Scott would rather we spend a month."

"A week should do it this time, Captain," Scott said, taking a spoonful of the savory soup. "They didn't tear the guts out of her and make us stuff them back in. Only minor modifications."

"Minor if you stayed out of sickbay for three weeks," McCoy said.

"I assume you were briefed on what's happened to the *Enterprise*," Kirk said.

"I was given an outline. I'm here to fill in the rest."

"Perhaps Mister Veblen could help," Spock said. Before him on the table was carafe of cloudy water. He poured a glassful and sipped it reflectively.

"Certainly," Veblen said. He was a short, chunky man with blond hair cut shorter than regulation length, a bulbous nose, and penetrating, elfishly-upslanted green eyes. He had come aboard the *Enterprise* the year before to coordinate the upcoming monitor installation, serving first as Spock's assistant and chief computer officer. Though Veblen didn't look like the most representative Starfleet

Academy graduate, Kirk had come to respect him—grudgingly, and with a healthy list of reservations. "The *Enterprise* is now outfitted with a Federation monitoring system. The Federation has been worried for years about the power of Starfleet vessels, and the possibilities of gross misuse, and not without justification . . . even within the captain's experience, as I've learned. There have been safeguards in the past, but nothing like these. The monitors are planned to eventually oversee all of ship operations. For this voyage, there are two basic systems—command, the largest, and medical, to oversee the new TEREC."

"Terec?" Mason asked.

"Transporter Emergency RECovery unit," McCoy explained.

"If and when the monitors decide that a Starfleet vessel is operating in a manner not beneficial to the Federation's interests," Veblen continued, "they will take over until the situation has been normalized, or until the *Enterprise* has withdrawn from her difficulties. The command monitors contain the experience memories of six past Starfleet commanders whom the Federation regarded as superior in all categories. These surrogates are now machine combinatorial personalities, checking and rechecking with each other—"

"Bridge to Captain Kirk. Uhura here, Captain. We have an urgent message from Starfleet."

"Is there any other kind?" McCoy grumbled.

"They request an immediate answer."

"I'll be right up, Lieutenant." He pushed his chair back from the table. "Excuse the interruption. Please proceed."

Mason felt a little shiver of anticipation. "They can't leave us alone even for the space of a good meal," McCoy said, shaking his head.

Chapter Four

In the time it took Kirk to reach the bridge—less than two minutes—Uhura had a heads-up projector ready, aimed at the captain's chair, and scrambled channels on subspace open for his reply. Kirk took his seat. In less than a second, he was deep into the dispatch. The heads-up display projected an image into his eyes alone, and bone-resonance speakers in his neck brace fed him audio.

BuUnexTerr HighPri Message, Relay Starbase 19, Capt. James T. Kirk ONLY. "Kirk."

He recognized the voice of Admiral Hiram Kawakami, in charge of Starfleet's Bureau of Unexplored Territory.

"Captain, we've received a status geometry message from Octant 7, Black Box Nebula Station One. It took ten years for that message to reach the nearest Federation automatic relay buoy."

"I thought the Black Box station had been written off years ago," Kirk muttered.

"The message is partly visual. Here it is, Jim."

A strong-featured Vulcan face, with the deeper greenish-tan caste common to a purebred member of one of the old families, appeared before him, surrounded by what looked like an orderly communications center aboard a slightly under-funded research station. The display identified the Vulcan in bright red letters as Grake, a physicist, husband to T'Prylla. T'Prylla was well known, one of the finest Vulcan physicists and, Jim believed, related in some way to his own science officer—though precisely how, he couldn't remember. Vulcan family ties could be very complicated.

Grake was speaking High Vulcan, which the language implant at the base of Kirk's skull translated, matching Grake's intonations perfectly.

"Had we not a strong suspicion of something amiss, we would not be sending this preliminary message. With three protostars entering the main sequence within the Black Box Nebula, all subspace communication has been disrupted. Nevertheless—"

The signal faded and Kawakami's voice returned.

"We have high-speed equipment transmission, along with the interrupted visual. Science channel on that MC is very interesting. We now have a great deal more information on which to base our opinion of the ultimate fate of the Black Box station. Switch to high-speed ingest, Captain."

Kirk mentally adjusted his implant. His mind was immediately flooded with information. He cringed slightly; in some ways he was more afraid of technology than McCoy, especially technology which messed with the inside of his head. The ache left by high-speed information absorption didn't endear the process to him. Nevertheless, in a few seconds he was able to sort out the key facts.

The conversion of the Black Box Nebula from a dark cloud to a starwomb had not been sufficiently violent to destroy the research station. The sudden silencing of the station, and the fusion ignition of the

25

infant stars, had inevitably been associated. Failure to re-establish contact had led Starfleet to send an unmanned rescue vessel to the nebula. When it disappeared without a trace, Starfleet deemed it inadvisable to mount a full-scale rescue mission—a decision Kirk personally had disagreed with. Still, he disliked second-guessing his superiors.

Grake's message was incomplete, but from his tone and manner, it seemed reasonable to assume that most of the station personnel—if not all—had survived. Still, there were unexplained problems. After the protostar ignition had run its course, the station should have been able to use sub-space. While there was a reference to high levels of Ybakra radiation in the science data, that couldn't interfere with sub-space unless there were previously uncharted sub-spacial mass anomalies in the area. It appeared the science data was incomplete, as well.

"Captain, most of the personnel aboard the station were kept in deep freeze. Our physicists say there's a strong possibility that Ybakra radiation from the vicinity of the collapsed protostars has degraded the myelin sheathing on the nerves of all frozen "sleepers" . . . and the Enterprise *is the only starship presently equipped to deal with such a medical emergency."*

Emergency! Not much of an emergency after ten years, Kirk thought. Still, if the sleepers hadn't been revived . . .

"Your orders are to proceed to the Black Box at maximum warp, relieve survivors—if any—and do a complete procedural and scientific investigation. All prior assignments are postponed. The Romulans and Kshatriyans have given permission for Enterprise *to cross neutral zones in their vicinity, up to star date 4386.5, after which time* Enterprise *will be regarded as hostile and fired upon."*

Cutting it close, Kirk thought. Even at Warp eleven, maximum without giving Scotty severe angina, it would take them two weeks to cross the galaxy into octant 7.

"Representatives from the Vulcan Spyorna have made their concern quite clear. T'Prylla is an extremely valuable Vulcan, Jim, even if something of a renegade."

The Admiral gave his formal sign-off as Kirk ordered all senior watch officers to the briefing room. He suggested Mason should be present. "Mr. Sulu to the bridge," he concluded, "and rig for prolonged warp maximum."

Mason took a seat in the corner of the room, watching the officers file in and making notes about their physical appearance and apparent mental states. One of the two FNS mobile recorders assigned to her for the story floated beside her, sensors and lenses extended. The recorder was an older model, a flat rectangular prism about fifty centimeters long and twenty wide.

When the senior watch officers had absorbed the information from the transmission, they sat attentively around the consoles and briefing table. Spock had lifted one eyebrow, seemingly for good, and intently examined a science display. McCoy made notes on his electronic scratchpad, while Scotty—much as Kirk had expected—shook his head and muttered.

"Any comments, gentlemen?" Kirk asked.

"Captain," Scott began.

"I am aware of condition of engineering, Mr. Scott," Kirk said. Then, softening, "But . . . I would appreciate an update."

"I was not expecting a prolonged warp maximum, Captain. E'en with our time in spacedock, we need at least a day at warp two for a Jeffries refit, or we could blow an entire bus in bottle seven. I've been nursing that one along until we could log travel time—it cannot be done stationary."

"Thank you, Mr. Scott. Where will we be when the refit becomes necessary?"

Scott looked distinctly uncomfortable. "We are seventeen days from the Black Box at maximum warp. If we go all out for the first part of our trip—"

"Which we will," Kirk said.

"Then we'll be right in the middle of the Kshatriyan neutral zone."

"Do what you can now. I'll give you four hours at warp two. We won't have the luxury later."

Scott knew better than to offer further argument. He nodded and stared darkly at his work forms.

McCoy was next. "The crew has been ridden hard, Jim. Our last mission was no piece of cake. Even with a month in drydock, we haven't had opportunity for liberty."

"So what can we do about it, Bones?"

McCoy shrugged. "Keep a stiff upper lip, as usual."

"Can we handle it?"

"Of course we can. But—"

"That's what I need to know. Mr. Spock, you're looking pensive."

Spock glanced up, eyebrow still raised. "The captain must be aware that I am a blood relative of T'Prylla."

"Yes. I'd like that clarified, Spock."

"She is my father's second brother's daughter by his fourth *trilya* marriage. She is married to a former pupil of my first discipline master. This situation presents an interesting dilemma, Captain. By now, both T'Prylla and Grake have been ceremonially interred and their social positions refilled. If they are alive, they will have to compete for a new social position—"

"Were they *mourned*, Spock?" McCoy asked sarcastically.

Spock raised his other eyebrow. "That is not the dilemma. Why should the *Spyorna* have any further interest in a Vulcan they have officially decreed to be *akspra*—the follower of an inadequate philosophy? It is my guess the *Spyorna* is about to recognize T'Prylla's kind of logic as useful. This could be very important to Vulcans, Captain; moreso if she is still alive and can guide us in our progress."

"That's very interesting, Spock, but I'm really interested in your assessment of the difficulties involved in reaching the station."

Spock assented with a nod to one side. "The Black Box Nebula is one of seven hundred collapsing nebulae accessible to us, Captain. It is by far the largest and most complex, principally because of the extreme turbidity within the nebula proper. The three newly created stars are likely to become hot, middle-size B-class stars. If, as surmised, there are sub-spacial mass anomalies nearby, in their early years they will have released a tremendous amount of Ybakra radiation. Such radiation operates in a fractional space and is not dangerous to normal carbon-based life forms—unless they are in a frozen state associated with suspended animation. Bodily defenses are then incapable of making the minute but constant repairs necessary to the myelin sheaths which act as insulation in both human and Vulcan nerves."

"Which is where I come in," McCoy said. "If the sleepers haven't been revived, the new equipment in the sick bay might be able to save them. But there's a problem, Jim—"

"Was that all, Spock?"

Mason sat quietly in her corner, noting the style of the meeting, and the often informal give-and-take between Kirk and his officers.

"No, Captain," Spock said, unperturbed. "We know very little about protostar formations of this sort, and with the silencing of the station in the Black Box, there have been no updates until now. The information relayed by the buoy is incomplete and highly inadequate. In short, the *Enterprise* will be entering unknown conditions, with unknown consequences."

"Yet again," McCoy said. "How cheering."

"You mentioned a problem, Doctor?"

"The equipment. It's easy enough to operate, even within the guidelines of those damned . . . excuse me, the guidelines of the monitors. It practically runs itself. But I don't think Starfleet has taken the monitors into account in evaluating this situation. The best way I can figure out to save the sleepers is to beam them up frozen, rescue their transient form-memories from the transporter and feed them into the vat, two by two. Mr. Veblen here will tell you the difficulties involved with computer storage of transient form-memories."

"Enormous difficulties, Captain," Lieutenant Veblen said.

"Such as, Mr. Veblen?"

"Transient form-memories are stored by a kind of quantum trick, Captain. There are well over a hundred and fifty million gigabytes of information needed to restore one human body after beaming. All of that is kept in fraction space storage for less than five minutes. It then deteriorates. Any attempt to re-beam from a deteriorated form-memory is disastrous. Until now, there were no facilities to provide a medical back-up for restoration with the failure of a transporter."

Kirk tapped his fingers on the table. Veblen saw, and swallowed back his expanding explanation. "Sir, we can store the memory of six transporter malfunction victims but we only have facilities to rebuild two at a time. To store any more, we'll have to use ship's computer memory, which operates on a different process entirely. If there are thirty sleepers on the station, we could put two of them per week into the TEREC. That would take—"

"Fifteen weeks."

"Which means we'd have to stay in orbit around

the planetoid for at least the time necessary to retrieve all the sleepers. Or we could dump the entire *Enterprise* library to store the form memories."

"Against regulations, Mr. Veblen."

"Precisely."

"Why not beam them up frozen, then beam each into the unit as his time comes?"

"There's the rub, Jim," McCoy said. "With radiation damage, we can only risk transporting them once. The second time, they're dead."

"Was that the problem with regs you mentioned?"

"No. Even if we do get them up here, we'll have to program changes into the vats to restore their myelin sheaths. The monitors may not let me do that. I told you I wasn't sure the regs made much sense."

"You told me you didn't want to be a lawyer. Is there any reason why we can't ferry the sleepers up in the shuttlecraft?"

"There could be risks," McCoy said. "Hibernacula require very stable power sources, and constant low temperatures. We may have to take the chance, but I wish we had other choices."

"Gentlemen, is there anything further I should know before we begin our rescue mission?"

"Very likely, Captain, there are a great many things you should know," Spock said. "None of which we are able to tell you."

Mason made a note of that, as well, and underlined it twice. "Captain," she said as the officers stood to return to their duties. "Since this is such an unusual mission, am I to be dropped off on my planet before you depart?"

Kirk hardly looked at her as he passed. "Not unless you directly request it."

She watched him follow Spock out of the briefing room door, mentally kicking herself. She couldn't back down now. The man was so arrogant! Why couldn't he have made it easier on her, instead of throwing the ball in her court? She'd show herself to be a complete coward, and if she did come back to Yalbo, word would get around . . . and she would be accused of shaming them all. In front of non-humans, too.

She gripped her notepad tightly, chewing on her lower lip and trying to still the nagging voice in the back of her mind, a voice saying she was too young, too inexperienced; saying that FNS had made a bad mistake sending her to the *Enterprise*.

Chapter Five

Kirk was eternally fascinated by the procedures for making the *Enterprise* ship-shape for a long voyage. He was as familiar with every action as a man watching his wife dress in the morning, and yet . . . it had that same sort of fascination, of responsibility mixed with a perverse and impossible kind of ownership. No individual could own a starship, any more than a man could actually own his wife. Still, the *Enterprise* was his. He wondered what the day would be like when he had to give her up, and whether, if any of his Starfleet colleagues assumed her command, they could possibly remain friends.

From the captain's chair, he watched preparations on the various displays accessible to him, the largest being the forward viewing screen. At the touch of his fingers—resting on buttons set into his chair arms— and at the sound of his voice, he could make the *Enterprise* come alive. Stroking . . .

He put such errant nonsense from his thoughts

(and a good thing neither Spock nor McCoy could read minds at a distance) and concentrated on a report from Scott. The preventive maintenance procedures had been completed in record time, though they would still need four hours at warp two for the Jeffries refit.

Scott had suggested that three of his engineering crew receive notes of commendation. Kirk composed the notes on his command console and directed they be entered into the ship's record and individual crew files; Scott's recommendations were as good as gold, as far as he was concerned.

The Andorran, Lieutenant Yimasa, came on the bridge and took his position in the navigator's chair.

"The *Enterprise* is responsive, Captain," Sulu said, turning to grin at Kirk.

"Yes, indeed," Kirk said. His crew should have been on the edge, exhausted, ready for at least a month of shoreleave—yet here they were, seemingly eager, almost chipper. He felt a flood of warmth behind his eyes and blinked the emotion back.

"Fix your bearings, Mr. Sulu, Mr. Yimasa. Await my command to exit spacedock."

"Bearings fixed, Captain."

McCoy stepped up behind Kirk's chair and laid his hand on his shoulder. "Jim," he said softly. "I want to talk to you about the Mason girl."

"What about her?"

"Are you sure it's best—"

"Bones, she's a professional. Besides, Starfleet ordered that we should cooperate with the FNS."

"Jim, she's an outposter. She wouldn't know her way around a small town, much less the *Enterprise,* much less the *Enterprise* on an emergency rescue mission."

"I don't foresee any danger. Do you, Bones?"

"Every time we go someplace there's that potential."

"True enough. What makes you think she can't handle herself?"

"Instinct. I may be wrong, but she just doesn't look comfortable. Have you seen the way she looks at Spock and Yimasa?"

"There are no non-humans on Yalbo. They may be the first she's ever seen."

"I suspect the FNS picked her because she was the only one they could slip on the *Enterprise* before the shakedown. So I'm making my suggestion for two reasons—"

"What suggestion?"

"That we put her down on Yalbo now. Two reasons, Jim. She's not up to it, and I'm not sure I'd want the responsibility if I were you."

"I left it up to her. If I put her planetside now, both FNS and Starfleet would pin my ears back. She's FNS's choice. I must assume they know what they're doing."

"Hmph." McCoy looked highly dubious. "Did you happen to read the last story FNS did on a Starfleet vessel?"

"No. I'm not much for the dailies, Bones."

"A correspondent from Mars spent two days aboard a heavy duty freighter. By the time he was through, he'd unveiled rampant corruption, the possible existence of an unknown space plague and the general incompetence of the captain. None of which charges, I might add, was regarded seriously by a special review board."

Kirk sighed. "Bones, she doesn't want to leave. I can't make her go. She has a job to do."

"Oh, she *wants* to leave; you just didn't give her any easy way out." McCoy's eyes widened. "Jim, you'd like her to stay, wouldn't you?"

Kirk regarded McCoy with a level stare. "Doctor, I have a ship to take out of spacedock. We can discuss this later, if you . . . haven't caught on by then." He turned his chair forward. McCoy straightened, shook his head and backed away a few steps. It was the doctor's policy to be on the bridge for the first hour or so of any voyage, whenever possible.

Nurse Chapel was in control of the sickbay, so he could indulge his little quirk.

"Engineering," Kirk said.

"Scott here, Captain."

"Outfitted and ready to sail, Mr. Scott?"

"Boilers at superheat, sir."

"Strain your gaskets, Mr. Scott."

"Aye, sir. Gaskets already strained."

Kirk smiled. "Dead slow, Mr. Sulu. Lieutenant Uhura, send our sincere thanks to the spacedock crew, and our compliments to the orbital advisory committee on Yalbo."

Mason came on the bridge, looking apprehensive. Her recorder followed at a discreet distance. She fixed her eyes on the forward screen and stood beside McCoy. "Are we leaving?" she asked.

"Yes, ma'am."

"How long before we use warp drive?"

"Not long at all."

"Impulse power, Mr. Sulu," Kirk said. "All ahead full."

"Aye, Captain."

The *Enterprise*, heir to three thousand years of human and Vulcan experience on sea, sand and in space, had exited the spacedock with majestic slowness. Now she gently stretched the gravitational bonds of Yalbo and spiraled outward, lining up with the corkscrew magnetic fields of Yalbo's small yellow sun. Kirk could feel the vibration of the impulse engines, smooth enough but always coarse when compared with the steady power of the warp drive.

"Aligned for solar system exit, sir," Yimasa said.

"Very well. Warp one, Mr. Sulu."

Kirk felt his chest strain at the sensation of the *Enterprise*'s sudden ignorance of gravitational bonds. She was now at the beck and call of a higher geometry, one which propelled her at just above the speed of light away from the tiny ochre planet of Yalbo, and away from her yellow star. Kirk briefly called up a virtual display of the outside view. The entire universe seemed compressed to a coruscating band of light, rotated and bent away from the direction of the view cameras. "Warp two and hold until Mr. Scott okays us for final warp sequencing," he said.

"Aye, Captain."

He switched the virtual display off. The forward screen now showed a computer simulated display of the stellar system and distant stars. When the *Enterprise* reached warp four, some of the closer stars themselves would appear to move on the display.

Kirk glanced at Mason, wondering if she was feeling what he felt. Like a tune in his bones, the warp drive sang, a beautiful siren pushing the ship faster in relation to status geometry—the home universe—yet retarding its speed in relation to the higher spaces they now traversed. The secret of the warp drive, in fact, was that it did not allow the *Enterprise* to reach an infinite speed in alien geometries, which would turn them all into a single tiny, very dead black hole.

"Welcome to warp drive, Mister Mason."

"Thank you, Captain. It's quite an experience." She wondered if she was going to be ill. And where was the science officer, the Vulcan? Wasn't he supposed to be on the bridge at a time like this? As if in psychic response, the elevator door opened and Spock stepped out, walking to his station at the computer console. Lieutenant Veblen followed, smiling at her in passing.

"At this speed, we'll exit your system in two hours," Kirk said. "I venture you've never traveled that fast before."

"I've never been off Yalbo until now. I'm just a country bumpkin, Captain." She was embarrassed by her own tone. "I hope to get sophisticated fast."

"Don't rush it, Mister Mason," Kirk said. "First experiences are to be savored."

"I'll savor them in my off-duty hours, Captain. And please call me Rowena."

"Certainly, Rowena. I see you've requested an interview with me in the ship's computer bay. Will 1600 hours be okay? If Scotty . . . Mr. Scott gets his refit done in time, we should be at warp maximum by then, and I can spare about fifteen minutes."

"I'll be there." She swallowed and decided she needed a place to sit down. Since there was no seat on the bridge not already taken, she returned to the elevator. As the doors closed, McCoy frowned and tapped his finger on the railing.

"Captain, Scott in engineering. We've finished the refit. She should take warp maximum without too many problems."

"What, no complete certainty?" Kirk asked.

"Nothing will go wrong that we won't be able to take care of," Scott said. "And if something does go wrong, you'll be the first to know. After us, Captain."

"Ready, Mr. Scott?"

"As we'll ever be."

"Good. Mr. Yimasa, final adjustment to bearings."

"Yes, sir. We'll exit the galactic arm in two hours ten seconds of ship's time. Catenary curve through four selected geometries as soon as we hit warp seven."

"Sequence us through warp five, Mr. Sulu."

"Sequencing."

The tune in his bones quickened its tempo.

"Three, Captain. Four. And . . . five."

"Sequence through warp eleven, Mr. Sulu. Mr. Yimasa, compute our entry point into Romulan neutral zone as soon as you can and put it on my console display."

"Warp six. Seven."

Kirk's eyes narrowed. "Eight," Sulu continued. "Nine. Ten. Maximum warp eleven, Captain."

Warp eleven was a special treat for James Kirk. The tune in his bones became a symphony. Secretly, he relished the thought of evading status geometry for seventeen days—even if the course did take them through contested territory. If they were lucky, they would spend less than an hour in the neutral zones . . .

That is, if they were not interfered with. He knew some of the Romulan and Kshatriyan commanders who patrolled those regions. Good officers, good commanders—and very anxious to test their abilities and their ships against his.

Ah, peace, he thought. Like seduction. Sometimes much more exciting than the act itself . . .

He made a mental note to set the sonic shower for a very cold cleansing before his next sleep period.

"What can you tell me about T'Prylla, Spock?"

Spock sat stolidly on his immaculate stone meditation plank, eyes closed, deep in the mathematical exercises he had taken up lately, conditional to his entry into the third stage of Vulcan life at age seventy-nine. Kirk knew he wasn't interrupting his friend; Vulcans had the remarkable ability to devote their attention to several things at once.

"She is a most extraordinary Vulcan, Captain. I regret not knowing her better. She has pioneered new ways of logic, ways heretofore regarded as unacceptable by the *Spyorna*. She mated outside of family pre-arrangements—"

"A tradition you've had difficulties with, if I recall," Kirk said ruefully.

Spock nodded his head to one side. "In my case, the contamination of human blood could be brought to account. But T'Prylla is pure Vulcan, and in many ways her approach harks back to a very famous Vulcan *Strovadorz*—a philosopher—named Skaren, who recommended the prevalence of inductive over deductive reasoning. Inductive reasoning is essential, but not a Vulcan's favorite."

"You're saying she uses feminine intuition?"

"A statement worthy of Dr. McCoy, Captain."

"Yes. My apologies. At the very least, she's been regarded as wayward."

"And quite brilliant. For Grake and T'Prylla not to have foreseen and prepared for the dangers of their research is highly unlikely. I must assume that something completely outside Vulcan and human experience has occurred in the Black Box Nebula. We must ready ourselves accordingly."

"How will we do that?"

"I have been studying Mr. Veblen's texts on the new computer systems. The principle of stochastic algorithm is quite intriguing. To set up a portion of the ship's computer which simply models possibility after possibility, always throwing in some unlikely variable, until it produces a situation which matches our own, could be quite helpful."

Kirk regarded the Vulcan for several minutes, thinking. In some ways, this was shaping up to be a routine rescue mission. But Spock's statements bothered him. They could certainly do worse than let Veblen loose—within limits. Kirk wasn't sure he trusted Veblen completely; he deviated from the Starfleet norm in much the same way Spock said T'Prylla deviated from the Vulcan norm. But setting aside a stochastic modeling program seemed reasonable enough.

"I'll get him working on it right away," Kirk said. He stood up. "We'll cross the Romulan neutral zone tomorrow at 1536 hours."

"1536 point 42," Spock said.

"Of course. Forgive my interruption."

"Krawkra," Spock said, a complex Vulcan term roughly equivalent to the Spanish *de nada*.

Chapter Six

The computer bay was a small room barely ten feet
on a side, located several decks beneath the bridge
in the *Enterprise*'s saucer. The ship's main computer
was lodged in the walls, which were little more than
an inch thick. The room was empty save for a
pedestal in the middle and a metal mesh pathway
leading to the pedestal. Mason stood on the pathway, notepad in hand, bemused by the complete
silence. Here, even the ineffable sensation of being
in warp drive was missing. Kirk stood by the pedestal, waiting patiently for her next question. They
were ten minutes into the interview and thus far
Kirk had given only a precis of his career, which she
had duly recorded, knowing she would have to go
elsewhere to flesh it out. "I suppose we should get
down to the inevitable."

"What might that be?" Kirk asked warily.

"How does a starship Captain feel, knowing that
his every decision is going to be second-guessed by a
machine?"

Kirk hated being diplomatic to the point of misleading, but this was clearly a time when evasion was necessary. "Starfleet has the interests of the Federation in mind. If a starship captain engages in erratic behavior, the monitors will act as a safeguard. They'll take away the captain's command. It's my duty not to be . . . erratic."

"Surely Starfleet is very careful in choosing its captains. Isn't it impossible for a man or woman who's passed all the tests to be a bad apple?"

Again she was leading him into delicate matters. Kirk knew of fellow officers who had "gone bad." They were rare, and the unfortunate results had never extended beyond damage to Starfleet vessels —and crew deaths—but there was always the possibility . . .

"It's never impossible for a human being to make a mistake. The monitors have been installed to catch me—us . . . if a mistake is made."

"But what if it's a difference of opinion, a judgment call, and you're not allowed to follow your own judgment?"

"That hasn't happened yet."

"The system hasn't been tried, Captain."

"True. But I dislike speculation. By the end of this mission, we should have enough experience to know whether modifications are necessary."

"Do you expect them to be?"

Kirk smiled. "No." I certainly hope not, he thought. "The monitors really consist of the experiences of six of our finest starship captains. It's much as if they were staring over my shoulder, offering friendly advice. I don't really expect to ever disagree with six of Starfleet's finest."

"Yes, but I'm sure no captain enjoys having his commands questioned by even the most brilliant of his peers. Isn't a captain supposed to be autonomous, the ruler of all the surveys?"

"A starship captain is part of a chain of command. He is never his own man." And how often had he strained that dictum past the breaking point?

"Sometimes the romance of command is overblown, wouldn't you say? I'm always accountable for my actions. In fact, I'm accountable for the actions of the *Enterprise* and all aboard her. If the monitors can help me in my work, I welcome them. Perhaps you should speak to Lieutenant Veblen. He can describe the technical details, those that aren't classified."

"That would be very useful. Is he available now?"

If he isn't, Kirk thought, I'll make him available. He motioned her out of the computer bay and called the computer control center, where Veblen was likely to be engaged in his endless checking and re-checking of the monitors' peripherals. "I'll need Mr. Veblen on the bridge with me in forty-five minutes," he told Mason. "Please don't keep him any longer than that."

"I won't," Mason said. She watched Kirk enter the elevator. She had learned nothing important —nothing she could substantiate, at any rate—and he had only given her thirteen minutes. But one thing was perfectly obvious to her, perhaps moreso than it was to Kirk himself. The captain of the *Enterprise* loathed the thought of being second-guessed.

Everything was running smoothly on the bridge. Kirk took his chair and paused before beginning an entry in the ship's log. Was it possible—barely possible—that the *Enterprise* could run herself better without him? He put the doubt aside almost before he had a chance to notice it, and made a routine status entry on the compact chair arm keypad. Veblen came on the bridge a moment later.

"Good day, Mr. Veblen," Kirk said. "I trust you had a pleasant interview with Mister Mason."

"Yes, indeed," Veblen said, smiling. "She's a very pleasant person. May I listen in on the monitors' communications with the command console, Captain?"

Kirk looked at him, vaguely irritated. "Yes. Of course." Veblen made the necessary patches through the science console and plugged in an earphone. His face assumed an air of blissful attentiveness as he listened to computer voices discoursing with each other in various machine languages.

"Mr. Veblen," Kirk said a few minutes later.

"Yes, Captain?" Veblen had plugged a diagnostic tricorder into the science console. The display on the console screens was spectacularly complex.

"Mr. Spock recommends that the *Enterprise* be prepared for any exigency, and I concur. We'll need—"

"Sir, I've already initiated a stochastic algorithm in the strategy and forecasting centers."

"Of course," Kirk said. He bit his lip. "Precisely. Any results yet?"

"It's only been running for an hour, sir." Veblen smiled almost gleefully. "Last I checked, it was running a model on the development of Hoyle clouds under protostar conditions."

"Hoyle clouds, Mister Veblen?"

"Large sentient masses of interstellar gas, Captain. Named after a twentieth-century astronomer."

"Yes. The *Enterprise* has encountered similar creatures several times. Why should that be amusing, Mr. Veblen?"

"By itself, no reason, sir. But the algorithm was speculating on the possibility they were chess masters." His smile widened, as if he were filled with some hidden joke he couldn't possibly explain.

"I assume that is in the nature of the algorithm, Mr. Veblen, and we shouldn't be alarmed?"

"Quite unnecessary, Captain. The program does not expect to be interrupted while preparing its required list of nonsense situations. It will select useful scenarios on its own."

"Thank you," Kirk said. Somehow his sense of humor faded when he was in the presence of the young computer officer. Perhaps it was Veblen's seeming inability to wear a uniform properly . . . "Please disengage the command console now, Mr. Veblen."

"Yes, sir." Veblen withdrew his tricorder and patches and returned the privacy of his chair to Kirk.

McCoy came on the bridge, looking mildly jubilant. He stood to one side of Kirk, smiled, and shook his head. "Captain, I think I've got the hang of working with the watchdogs. I'm learning to reason with them, God help me. We shouldn't expect too much trouble." He lowered his voice. "Unless we run into anything just the tiniest bit unusual." He cast a meaningful glance at Veblen.

"Glad to hear it, Doctor. When you've mastered them, perhaps you'll inform me how to deal with Mr. Veblen's command override."

"That's simple, Jim," McCoy said. "Just don't screw up. Use your own judgment, but for God's sake don't make any decisions."

Kirk laughed. "Status report on your weapons tests, Mr. Chekov."

Chekov swiveled his chair. "We are ready for almost anything, Captain."

Captain's Log, Stardate 4380.4.

I'm going back through my tapes and trying to find all the information on hand about Kshatriyan Vice Commodore Uligbar Dar Zotzchen. VC Dar Zotzchen is the last confirmed commander of the Kshatriyan stretch of the neutral zone. As anticipated, the Romulans gave us no trouble during our brief passage; the Kshatriyans, however, are not likely to be so cooperative, even with the acquiescence of their Federation representatives.

I last had dealings with Dar Zotzchen when I was a very green exec aboard the *Bonne Homme Richard,* escorting treaty software to the presiding regent Dom Hauk. My impression was that VC Dar Zotzchen is a devious son of a bitch, and nobody to trust when you're in a hurry—

INTERRUPT / INTERRUPT / INTERRUPT / INTERRUPT / INTER

Kirk was on the bridge in less than a minute. Veblen smoothly disengaged the command override, which thankfully had done nothing in the meantime, and Uhura played back the message.

Kirk listened intently. Yes, indeed, the voice—even in translation—was that of Dar Zotzchen. Unforgettable.

"Defender of the Kshatriyan God's Endowment, Prime Commodore Uligbar Dar Zotzchen to the inept commander of the easily recognizable Federation starship *Enterprise*. Your course will take you across Kshatriyan neutral territory. That is regarded as an act of war. Are you prepared to violate all that our treaties stand for?"

"Greetings," Kirk said, "to the Righteous Defender Dar Zotzchen. Congratulations on your promotion, and all proper respect to the Presiding Regent." Kirk deliberately left out the regent's name, in case there had been reshuffling in the royal house. "The Prime Commodore's servant officers must be lax in their duties, not to inform His Vigilance that we have already sought and received permission to cross. We are on a rescue mission."

Uhura listened closely, then swung her chair around to face Kirk. "There is no reply, Captain."

"Sir," Veblen said, "the monitors suggest the Kshatriyan will probably broadcast a conciliatory reply on an obscure channel to—"

"Lieutenant Uhura and I are quite aware of that, Mister," Kirk said, perhaps too sharply. "Lieutenant, repeat my signal, and add the substance of the message from the Kshatriyans granting Starfleet permission."

Spock came on the bridge, took his position at the science center, and surreptitiously checked on Veb-

46

len's points of access to the computers. Kirk noticed this and smiled his appreciation. He didn't like being in a conspiracy against one of his own officers, but in a possible emergency, it was best to know everything in advance—including whether the new systems would allow him a full range of actions.

Mason came on the bridge a moment later. Her expression was more harried than scared, but this changed to stiff-faced control as she caught on to the situation.

"Still no reply, Captain," Uhura said, glancing back at her new roommate.

"Distance to the neutral zone, Mr. Yimasa."

"Three light hours and closing rapidly, Captain."

"Maintain warp maximum. Ensign Chekov, load torpedo bays with decoy targets and prepare to launch. Shields on maximum."

"Reply coming in now, Captain."

"Let's hear it."

"Captain Kirk, is it not?" The Kshatriyan had altered his tone to take advantage of human inflections. "Our records are not so precise, but I remember a young officer with a voice very much like your own. I assume you have achieved your own command, and my congratulations. I measured you as a worthy adversary then, despite your inexperience. Our machines are even now searching for such a message. Until then, please reduce to impulse power and skirt the neutral zone."

Kirk grimaced. "Reply, Lieutenant: Unable to reduce to sub-lightspeed. Repeat, we are on a rescue mission and time is of the essence. We have already broadcast your own government's response, complete with uniquely coded identifiers. Please allow us to pass. Your hostility could be considered the first step toward a very undesirable situation."

Uhura listened for a few minutes. The bridge was silent, except for Mason's somewhat uneven breathing. Kirk looked at Veblen and saw flushed excitement on his face, but no fear. Mason was beginning

47

to show her distress in various twitches and nervous motions.

"No reply, Captain."

"Maintain warp maximum, Mr. Sulu. Mr. Chekov, clear the bays of two decoys and load two photon torpedos. Do we have the Kshatriyan ships, Mr. Yimasa?"

"They are still out of range and hiding, sir."

"Sir—" Veblen said.

"No interruptions, please, Mr. Veblen."

"But this could be important, sir—"

For God's sake, Mason wanted to scream, listen to him!

"Please!" Kirk shot an angry glance at the computer officer, who nodded and backed away a step. "Distance, Mr. Yimasa."

"Two light hours from neutral zone buoy eighty-one, the closest, sir."

"Yellow alert, gentlemen." The sirens began on all decks. "General quarters." There was a piercing whistle, and a mechanical echo of his command. On his console, a display ticked off the stations reporting fully manned and ready. The bridge screen showed a reconstructed image of the stars immediately ahead, and postulated positions of the Kshatriyan battle fleet.

"We have them, Captain," Chekov said. Yimasa concurred. "They are in the classic Warp-E formation. They look very combative."

Kirk nodded. The green postulated positions of the fleet on the forward screen were replaced by red confirmeds. In the Warp-E, the outlying lines of ships would be in warp drive, traveling between warp minimum and warp three, while a rear line and center piercing line were on impulse power. If the *Enterprise* were caught in that formation, no matter what tactic she used, she would be confronting fully prepared ships. Kirk saw that McCoy had come on the bridge. He stood near Mason, hands gripping a railing, wearing his tailored expression of overbearing interest.

"Mr. Sulu," Kirk said. He paused. Sulu turned, waiting. "Maintain course, steady as she goes."

"Sir, we will pass within range of their formation," Yimasa said.

"I assumed as much, Mr. Yimasa. Any signals, Uhura?"

"None, Captain."

"Steady, then. Steady." He sounded as if he were reassuring a horse, Mason thought. Kirk patted the chair arms and stared intently at the forward screen. Veblen stood to one side, trying to look chastened and not entirely succeeding.

It was at a time like this that Kirk felt he was almost in telepathic communication with Spock. The science officer's mere presence was enough to make Kirk believe that, somehow, he was doing what Spock would suggest.

"Fifty-seven light minutes."

"Status report."

"All stations manned and ready, Captain."

"Conditional red alert." Again the sirens, and the ticking off of acknowledgements on his command console.

Always the rush of adrenaline, which the caveman had used to prepare for the wolf or cave bear . . . and which Kirk was now using to prepare himself for a fleet of high-technology battle cruisers, deep between the stars, between dimensions.

Veblen swallowed audibly. His first time, Kirk thought. Good for him. Mason hadn't moved. She kept glancing between Kirk, Spock and McCoy.

"No reply, Captain," Uhura repeated.

"Spock, are we tapping their ship-to-ship?"

"Yes, Captain. They do not appear to be in a state of great alarm. Other than that, I cannot read the signals clearly. They may be false."

If that Kshatriyan son of a bitch was making him

49

put his crew through a conditional red, just to get his jollies . . .

"Two light-minutes," Yimasa said. "Within range."

"Warp-E shearing and closing," Chekov said.

"Full red alert," Kirk ordered.

"Impulse ships going to warp minimum," Chekov said.

"Formation closing on us, sir," Sulu reported.

"Prepare for combat, damage alert imminent."

"Captain!" Uhura held her hand to her ear. "A message from the Prime Commodore. He wishes us the best of Creator's luck, and acknowledges receipt of our permission to pass through the neutral zone . . ."

Kirk, McCoy and Mason let out their breaths at almost the same time. Kirk looked at the computer officer with a wry grin. "Well, Mr. Veblen?"

"Captain?"

"What did the monitors suggest?"

"That we shouldn't worry, sir. The Kshatriyans are unable to engage in a full-scale war at this time, have no need to do so and are renowned for enjoying testing their adversaries. The monitors concurred down the line with your actions, sir."

"Very glad to hear that, Mr. Veblen. Why was the message so urgent, then?"

"Why, sir, I felt there was no need for tension, if all was to go well. Wasted energy."

"Quite, Mr. Veblen," Kirk said, glancing at Mason. "Quite."

Chapter Seven

When Mason entered Uhura's quarters, the communications officer had just come off duty and was changing into a flowing orange and red robe, decorated with a fringe of leopards stalking through jungle grass. Uhura smiled at her and offered a glass of wine from the cabin autochef.

"That was really something," Mason said, sitting on the edge of her bunk. "I'm not sure I've ever been more scared."

"It was a bluff," Uhura said. "I think most of us were aware of that. I'm sorry there wasn't more time to prepare you."

"The captain didn't behave like it was a bluff."

Uhura laughed. "Poker face."

"And everybody seemed relieved when it was over."

"Well, you can never tell what a Kshatriyan might do. Do you know much about them?"

Mason shook her head. "Only what I've read in my schoolbooks and picked up from the subspace bulletins. The dailies."

"They're quite an admirable race, actually. Very tough, very defensive . . . and well they should be. They remind me of the Zulu. They're an old race, surrounded by the Romulans and the Federation, threatened by the Klingons . . . and still they hold their own, even against better technologies."

"They're the same basic stock as Commander Spock, aren't they?"

"They're part of the third octant Dakhrian migrations, if that's what you mean. The Vulcans, Romulans, Klingons and Kshatriyans are all related if you go back far enough."

"And Spock doesn't feel funny, siding with humans against his own blood?"

"I'm afraid the ties go too far back for any of them to feel much kinship. Besides, who knows what Spock *feels?*"

"I don't understand."

Uhura gathered up her gown and pulled a chair near to Mason's bed. "He's a Vulcan. They have very rigid codes governing emotions."

"Yes, I know that." She felt slightly irritated. "We're not *that* isolated on Yalbo. But doesn't he hold opinions?"

"Not unless there's a lot of evidence behind them. Personal opinions are anathema to a Vulcan. In fact, anything having to do with petty personal traits is subdued during Vulcan education. But enough talk about Spock. I'd like to learn more about you."

Mason shrugged. "I'm a reporter. I come from a very small, isolated planet. What else is there to say? Besides, I'm not important. Only the story."

"I'm sorry none of us could get down to Yalbo," Uhura said. "I like to visit all sorts of planets, even small ones."

"It started out as a mining colony," Mason said, one hand stroking the back of the other. She looked down at her hands and clasped them. "Full of metals, rare earths . . . We can't drink the groundwater. It would poison us. The atmosphere is filled with nitric acid vapor. When we go outside the compounds, we have to wear full body suits. It's not what you call a paradise."

"Still, I bet you like it." Uhura leaned forward, her dark eyes glittering. Mason grinned and shook her head.

"We all like something about where we grow up."

"The people, maybe?"

"Sure. There are good people on Yalbo."

"You're proud of Yalbo. Admit it."

Mason considered. "Of course. We've done some really remarkable things there. Like, we stayed alive until the Federation chose us for an outpost. That wasn't easy. Yalbo became productive just when there was a metals glut in the second octant. We'd have had to ship our output a thousand parsecs to even begin to be competitive. Those were hard times."

"How old were you?"

"Oh, I hadn't even been born then. But my parents told me all about them. Some people would have starved if it hadn't been for Starfleet rescue ships."

"My father served on a rescue ship," Uhura said. "Maybe he came to Yalbo."

"Accepting charity was hard. My people were Hippies, you know. They wanted to be self-sufficient, to get away from the Galactic government and set up their own commune. Most came from the Martian mining towns originally. They needed the rescue ships, but they weren't glad to see them. We never have approved of military venturing."

"I thought Hippies were from the 20th century."

"Communes on Mars started them up again. People on Yalbo changed a lot of things. We're Humanists. We believe that everything in the Galaxy centers on human beings, and that all other species are subordinate."

Uhura made a face. "Doesn't sound like a very useful philosophy."

53

"It works well enough on a planet where there aren't any other species. And you have to admit, somebody like Spock takes a little getting used to."

Uhura stood and folded her arms. "Rowena, I don't suggest you try to apply Yalbo philosophies on a starship. We've been too many places, seen too many things. If you really want to know what we're all about, you might spend some time going through the ship's open log." She paused, then bent over the reporter. "I've met non-humans who make us look like worms. We crawl into their sight, and crawl out again, and the only reason they don't step on us is they aren't at all *like* us. Humans aren't the center of anything."

"I'm sorry," Mason said. "I don't have anything against other species, but I do believe humans are important."

"Important, yes. More important, no. Now let me get down off my soapbox and fix us some dinner. What would you like?"

They ate quietly, a little wary of each other. When the sleep period was over, Uhura rose and sprayed on her uniform in the cabin sonic shower. She stood by the door as Mason dressed. "I have the bridge watch until 1800 hours. Come by just before then and I'll show you what I do. Then we can catch dinner in the mess and watch some entertainments in the wardroom."

"Uhura," Mason said as the lieutenant was about to leave.

"Yes?"

"Do you have trouble sleeping during warp?"

"Heavens, no. Why?"

"Just wondering." Perhaps it was being away from Yalbo, away from the smells and company of the compounds. She felt so alone, so very much among strangers. If she let it, her isolation could easily depress her and begin to affect her work, and she would never stand for that.

And she was angry. Uhura was human; whatever

54

her experiences, surely she felt more allegiance for humans than for other species! How would any species survive if it didn't feel more allegiance for its own kind? Did everyone on the *Enterprise* think Humanists were backwater reactionaries?

She checked over her equipment. Perhaps it wasn't a bad idea to do some research in the ship's open log. She had fifteen more days before the *Enterprise* reached the Black Box, time in which to steep herself in the lore of Starfleet, in the history of the *Enterprise*—time in which to find a chink in all that self-righteous military armor.

Chapter Eight

*WARNING! YOU ARE ENCROACHING UPON
SECURITY SECTOR! UNAUTHORIZED
ENTRY MAY RESULT IN PROSECUTION—*

Spock sat before the monitors console in the computer control center and regarded the message on the screen with mild distaste. As far as he and Veblen had been able to tell, there was nothing against Starfleet regulations—or even against the monitors' codes—in what he was about to do. Still, the human designers had studded every aspect of the monitors' programming with warnings and ambiguous threats. He knew a way around the warning—a path was charted in the system instructions themselves—so he erased the screen and proceeded into the heart of the system, the memory banks which contained the experience memories of six Starfleet commanders.

Of the six, four were now dead and two had retired from active duty. One of the dead was a

Vulcan, the only Vulcan to ever reach command rank in Starfleet, Admiral Harauk. Spock was very interested in Harauk's thoughts on certain matters, and from what he could tell, the monitors were perfectly capable of replicating Harauk to a certain degree. So long as Spock did not attempt to change the memory or tamper with the system in any way which would affect its function, the worst he was doing was affronting the monitors' sense of dignity—which was how he characterized the intent behind the messages. (Machines as complex as the monitors were often best dealt with in terms of quirks and personalities, especially when they had been designed by human beings.)

WARNING! MONITORS NOT DESIGNED TO OPERATE WITH INPUT OF ONE EXPERIENCE-MEMORY ALONE. MAY RESULT IN—

Spock cleared the screen again and placed the direct com earphones over his head. He heard a distant hissing noise—not interference but the carrier signal for the memory frequencies of Admiral Harauk. At this point, there was no need for a machine language interface. Spock pressed a button actuating voice communication and said, "Live long and prosper, Admiral Harauk. I am Spock, son of Sarek of Vulcan and Amanda Grayson of Earth. I am science and first officer aboard the U.S.S. *Enterprise.*"

"Live long and prosper, Spock," came the reply. Harauk's voice was steady and even, though a little tinny. "Have the monitors been activated?"

"No, sir, they have not. I am asking questions of my own initiative."

"To what end, Spock?"

"The Admiral is well aware that the first concern of a Vulcan is his duty. My commanding officer is a human, Captain James T. Kirk. The humans have created and installed the monitors aboard Starfleet vessels, but I am not convinced they have used the greatest wisdom in doing so."

"Still, it is your duty to follow Starfleet regulations, as I do."

"And I will. But I also have a duty to my captain, a duty to discover whether or not the monitors will hinder his performance. And . . . I am interested in a Vulcan's response to the monitors."

"I cannot communicate to you as Vulcan to Vulcan, Spock. I am not alive in this system, I am merely an advisory program."

"It is advice that I have come for."

"Humans have been known for erratic behavior. At their best, they are less disciplined than even an inadequate Vulcan. They have created the monitors to circumvent possible difficulties with their own kind. I see nothing wrong with the idea in principle."

"But in execution?"

"I am not aware of the actual functioning of the system. Vulcans were involved in its creation, and the very best human designers worked hard on it for years. Still, it must be obvious that I approve of the idea in principle, since I agreed to be part of the system."

"And if a situation should arise which is outside the experience of the monitors—outside of the experience of the advisory programs?"

"That possibility has surely been taken into account. It is obvious that a starship commander will encounter unfamiliar situations."

Spock thought for a moment. "I am worried. The system has never proven itself in actual use, and I do not believe we are going into an ideal situation for such a test."

"Then there is only one thing for you to do."

"Yes?"

"Your duty is foremost."

"I am well aware of that, Admiral."

"Your duty is foremost."

No matter how Spock phrased and rephrased his questions, that was the only answer Harauk's experience memories could give. This was far from reassuring. Which duty was Harauk referring to—duty to captain, ship, Starfleet? Duty to obey the monitors?

No Vulcan supported a creed that bound him to self-destruction without purpose, or the destruction of others for the sake of duty alone. Obviously, Harauk's experience memory was trying to impress upon him the necessity of a hierarchy of duties. Among Vulcans, such a hierarchy was seldom necessary. But among humans, in this situation—

WARNING! THE CORRECT USE OF THE MONITORS DEPENDS UPON THE INTERACTION OF THE SIX EXPERIENCE MEMORIES CONTAINED WITHIN THE SYSTEM.

Spock returned the monitors to their normal mode and removed the direct com headphones. The door to the computer control center beeped and Veblen entered with a notepad in hand, busily making calculations. "Mr. Spock! You might be able to answer a question—"

"And you, Mr. Veblen, might be able to answer one as well."

Veblen stopped and stared at Spock, obviously nonplused. "Anything you wish, Mr. Spock."

"Your question first."

"Oh, it'll wait." Veblen was intrigued by the very possibility that the science officer would have a question to ask of him.

"I have not yet had an opportunity to study the monitors' failsafe operations. If they should malfunction, in the estimation of the officers and crew of a vessel, can they be disengaged?"

"Such a failure is highly unlikely, sir."

59

"That does not answer my question."

"I . . . don't know myself, sir."

"Then it is time we studied the failsafes in more detail, wouldn't you say?"

Veblen regarded Spock shrewdly. "Sir, if I may ask another question entirely—what is it you expect us to find in the Black Box?"

"I am like the Federation Interstellar Scouts, Mr. Veblen. I believe it is necessary to be prepared."

Mason had spent her life in the compounds of Yalbo, and did not find the corridors and spaces of the *Enterprise* completely unfamiliar. Still, there was something about the size of an enclosed, self-contained ship like the *Enterprise* which was awesome. There were few areas of the ship off-limits to her, and even fewer reaches where she was not allowed to go for reasons of safety, at least with an escort, so exploring became one of her favorite past-times.

Even as a child, she had been fascinated by the recesses of the compounds, places where unused equipment was stored, or where the automated processing plants hummed and chugged in lonely efficiency. When Ensign Chekov procured a plastic map of the ship for her, she looked forward to days of walking, crawling, climbing. With the story foremost in her mind, however, she visited the sickbay first.

Nurse Christine Chapel—an efficient, somewhat spinsterish woman still firmly holding on to her classic beauty—showed her the diagnostic beds, both older and newer models, and explained the organ farm. The organ farm—official name, the Genotype Conservancy Center—was a large bank of shiny gray cabinets at the rear of the sickbay. "It's the forerunner to the TEREC unit," Chapel explained. "We have genetic records on hand for every member of the crew. In case of injury, we can grow a new replacement for any body part—except, of course, those which are deeply personalized, like the brain. We can grow a brain, but it will be quite blank. The major advancement in the TEREC is that we can replicate the present individual. And while you're here, you might as well make your contribution . . ."

With her fear of needles, it took some self-control not to protest when Chapel brought out a biopsy tomer. The nurse deftly and painlessly removed a section of cells from the inside of her cheek and closed the tiny gap with an electronic suture.

"We'll put this in the organ farm, and—heaven forbid!—if anything unfortunate happens, you'll have some insurance on file."

Chapel thought it would be best if McCoy gave her a tour of the TEREC itself, and McCoy was busy "playing poker with the monitors," as Chapel described it. "He's like a cardshark with a new victim. He should be human again in a few days."

Is it possible the Enterprise *personnel are taking delight in finding ways to circumvent the monitors?* Mason wrote in her notepad.

On some of her sojourns, she brought along the FNS recorder and made short documentaries of various ship activities. She expended an entire fifteen minutes of recorder file time on games played by the crew in the gym. *Highly competitive,* she noted, *the* Enterprise *crewmembers take delight in testing each other, and exhibiting their own prowess. While there is little* braggadocio, *per se, there is a firm commitment to doing one's best in all circumstances. In team activity, the degree of cooperation is impressive. Teams can be reshuffled at will, and yet the players mesh instantly and seamlessly, as if they have been mates all their lives—as indeed they have, where shipboard lives are concerned.*

Chief Engineer Scott was only too glad to show off the engineering decks. During an hour off duty, he took her on a single-minded "spelunking expedition" (his term) through the access tubes and maintenance corridors of the ship's impulse power plant. She held her hand, at his insistence, on the outer shield of one of the huge, oblate "bottles" where matter and antimatter were precisely mixed, and felt the indescribable tingle of controlled total destruction. She recorded—though she knew it would never pass FNS muster—his technical description of power plant theory, but was more interested in his summing up. "We could travel from one end of the universe to the other, if we could only fine tune our understanding of what we already have . . ." He shook his head and smiled. "She's a lovely engine, but I've seen engines on alien ships which make her look like a bicycle chain, and I'm the monkey pedaling. What I wouldna ha' gi'en just to peek at the manuals o' one of those!"

When McCoy finally got around to showing her the TEREC, she was somewhat disappointed. The doctor explained the basic operation of the unit, and touched briefly on how it was integrated with the monitors, but smiled when Mason asked if he believed the monitors would cause him difficulties.

"I'm working on it." he said, and would say no more.

While Spock and McCoy tried to understand the function of the monitors, and while Mason toured and took notes, the starship *Enterprise* rode a shockwave of warped spacetime above and through ribbons of stars and interstellar gas clouds, across galactic arms and obscured abysses, at speeds too great to be entirely real. Through the mysteries of advanced physics, she shed her natural tardiness in scattered, dissipating ghosts and sleeked across realms incomprehensible to the minds of most of those inside her hull.

Within two weeks, sensors could easily reconstruct the looming shape of the Black Box Nebula, no longer entirely dark. Mason, looking at the nebula on the screen in Uhura's cabin, thought she detected a sinister resemblance in the nebula's new aspect.

Where the light of the protostars shined through, it outlined three distinct, clawed talons. As the *Enterprise* approached, hour by hour the talons seemed to spread wider.

Then the reaches of the nebula closed around them, and the *Enterprise* and her crew were drawn back to genesis itself.

Chapter Nine

Station One was now embedded in a twisted strand of gas and dust at the nebula's perimeter. The *Enterprise* advanced through the clouds at less than one quarter lightspeed; any faster, and the buffeting of the diffuse nebula material would be dangerous. Uhura attempted to contact the station numerous times, without result. The nebula's brilliant shapes and patterns, seen from several dozen light years out, were now reduced to a constant transparent glow which bathed the *Enterprise* in dreamlike purple light.

Kirk examined the readouts on the forward screen, not at all happy with what he saw. Spock stood at his side. The *Enterprise* was on alert and the bridge was fully crewed. Mason stood near the elevator, recorder hovering nearby. "It looks like we've come here for nothing," Kirk said. Spock did not disagree. Graphs laid over the display of the tiny planetoid which had once held Station One showed no signs of life whatsoever, and the *Enterprise* had scanned the world from all sides.

"Unless there was a failure in the life support systems of the station itself," Spock said, "the condition of the planetoid gives us no reason to suspect any further harm could have come to them."

"Then maybe they're shy," McCoy said.

"Serious suggestions are what I need now, Bones." He glanced at Mason and was annoyed to find her noting his words on her pad. He was annoyed, in fact, that he was being recorded at all, but as McCoy had said often since their journey began, he alone was to blame for Mason's presence. He could have defied Starfleet; it probably would have resulted in a fracas, hard words here and there, but he would have prevailed. No; he strongly suspected that he had an ulterior motive for wanting her aboard. If the monitors failed miserably, an objective observer would record the failure.

And if *he* failed miserably—

McCoy was in the middle of a sentence when Kirk resumed listening. "—so I concur with Spock. There's no evidence the environment in the nebula was any harsher after the ignition than during."

"Mr. Veblen," Kirk said. The computer officer stepped forward smartly. "What do our computers say?"

"If you're asking for the results of the stochastic algorithm—"

"I am."

"I haven't had much time to enter these findings, sir. I can do so, and the algorithm can be re-selected."

"I'm curious to know what the algorithm came up with before we arrived."

"Sir, three possibilities were presented. Two were clearly in error—"

"Oh? Spock?"

"Mr. Veblen is referring to deviants which the computers themselves later rejected as unlikely. One referred to the take-over of the station by an outside force. The other considered the madness and suicide of all the station members. Neither of these possibilities were taken seriously in the final selection."

"The third scenario is quite interesting, Captain," Veblen said. "One or more of the Vulcan researchers aboard the station has been affected by the Ybakra radiation—"

"Vulcans are less capable of adapting to heavy doses of Ybakra," Spock said, "just as they are not as well suited to cold as humans are. Still, the differences are minor."

"—and has suffered a mental breakdown. The scenario diverges at this point. Either the other members of the team have been imprisoned, or—and this could be more likely, if we adjust the algorithm to the new findings—they have been murdered."

Kirk frowned. "I'm not sure I like your algorithm, Mr. Veblen. Spock, let's sweep the planetoid again. After that, a boarding party will assemble with full environmental gear and portable shields in the main transporter room."

"May I go down with you?" Mason asked. Kirk looked at her sharply.

"No," he said. "I'm not going down with the first team. Starfleet frowns on its commanders taking unnecessary risks. You may instruct one of the party in the use of your recorder, but we will not be responsible if it is lost or damaged."

Mason nodded, somewhat relieved.

With the failure of the final sweep to locate any signs of life, Kirk met the boarding party in the transporter preparation area. The party consisted of six crewmembers, headed by the chief of security, Lieutenant Olaus. Mason's recorder followed Olaus rather like a puppy; Olaus regarded the device with amused embarrassment as Mason tuned and adjusted it for its new task.

"This is to be a quick reconnaissance," Kirk said. "Mr. Devereaux will take tricorder readings and Mr. Mason's recorder will back up our observations. You will be down for less than two minutes; after that, you will automatically be returned to ship. Any one of you can signal for immediate return. You will be preceded by a transporter test device, as usual. Mr. Shallert, release the TTD. Mr. Olaus, assemble your team in the transporter."

The TTD was beamed down first and reported that the interior of the station was environmentally normal, and that the area appeared deserted. "Temperature is twenty-nine degrees celsius, Captain," Shallert reported from the transporter controls. "Oxygen level twenty-three percent, all other gases as expected for an operating life support system."

Spock advanced to Kirk's side. "The higher temperature is quite comfortable for Vulcans, Captain."

"Yes. Mr. Shallert, beam them down."

The transporter wrapped the shapes of the party members in pulsing lines of disintegration, mapping and disassembling their bodies. Gradually, the lines shrank and the shapes were reduced to nothing. Shallert checked the stored form-memories, then pulled the sliding switch which beamed them across five hundred kilometers to the interior of Station One.

"Could the station still be operating if all the researchers are dead?" Mason asked Kirk.

"It's conceivable," he said. "But not likely."

"Then why haven't you picked up any life signs?"

"We'll know a lot more in just a few minutes," Kirk said. "Patience is a virtue. Right, Spock?"

Spock stared stoically at the transporter control displays. "Arrival signal has been sent," he said. "They are in the station."

Chapter Ten

A warm breeze pushed quietly through the empty corridor. After ten years, the station was immaculate, everything in order, as if waiting for its guests to arrive.

And arrive they did, in six beautiful columns of structured fire, lighting up the utilitarian gray walls and adding a faint electric smell to the clean, dry air.

"Fan out," Olaus ordered. The team spread rapidly up and down the corridor, Ensign Devereaux aiming his tricorder in the prescribed patterns. Mason's recorder stayed close to Olaus, humming faintly. Olaus flipped open his communicator. "Landing party to *Enterprise*, Olaus reporting. Station appears to be in good shape. No signs of damage. Devereaux scanning. One minute thirty until return." He closed the communicator and inserted it into his belt. "Let's move!"

The six ran in two groups of three to each end of the corridor. At one end, where Olaus stood at ready, was a door leading into a storage chamber. The door was secured but not locked. At the opposite end, the corridor branched into a T, each subsequent hallway ending in a bulkhead with an airtight hatch. Devereaux advanced quickly to the left end of the T and punched a standard code into the hatch controls. The hatch sighed and slid open. He aimed his tricorder into the space beyond—

And narrowly missed the head of a young Vulcan boy.

"Hello," Radak said in perfect Federation English.

Devereaux stared at him in astonishment. "Lieutenant!" he called out, stepping back. "Lieutenant Olaus!"

Radak held out his hands in greeting, but the transporter effect had already begun. Their time was up; again, they were transformed into pillars of fire and pulled back aboard the *Enterprise,* as if they had been attached by a flexible string. The transporter grouped them together as they had left, but Devereaux was hunched slightly, tricorder held out, and Olaus had been caught in mid-run. He bounded from the platform and into Mason before he could recover. As he apologized, Mason's recorder switched its allegiance and returned to its former master, still humming.

"There's a Vulcan child in the station!" Devereaux said. "He speaks English—or, at least he said hello." Spock gently removed Devereaux's tricorder from his hands and played back the science data.

"Your device shows no Vulcan, child or otherwise," Spock said. "Who else saw the child?"

"I saw someone standing beyond Devereaux," said another member of the party. "But I couldn't see him clearly."

Spock adjusted the tricorder and still came up with negative results. "Mister Devereaux, please describe this Vulcan child."

"I'm no expert, Mr. Spock, but he seemed about twelve Earth years old, dark purple eyes, wearing a green uniform of some sort. He looked a bit like you."

Spock lifted an eyebrow and glanced at Kirk. "The tricorder shows no life other than the landing party. I cannot presume Mr. Devereaux was hallucinating, Captain, because T'Prylla's son, Radak, would be about fifteen Earth years old, and has dark purple eyes, unusual for a pure Vulcan. The landing party was issued no specific descriptions of station personnel."

Mason scanned the contents of the recorder's immediate memory. "It was with the wrong guy," she said. "It should have been with Devereaux. There's nothing on visual and if anybody said anything besides the landing party, I can't hear it. I might be able to pull it out after enhancement—"

"No need," Spock said. "The tricorder picked up no sound waves except those from the landing party. Nor was there any extra infrared or microwave radiation in the corridor, as might be expected if an actual living body had presented itself to Ensign Devereaux."

"So I *was* seeing things?" Devereaux asked, chagrined.

"Not necessarily," Kirk said. "I'll expect your reports in fifteen minutes in my quarters annex. Mr. Spock, I'll want you and Doctor McCoy . . . and Mr. Veblen . . . there in fifteen minutes, also." He turned to Mason. "You're welcome to come, needless to say."

"I wouldn't miss it," Mason said. "A haunted station . . . wouldn't miss it for a lifetime supply of filters."

For the first time in nine years, Grake became aware of a separate existence. He looked down at his body and stretched out his arms, then brought his hands closer to his face. Oh, yes, there were memories . . . but the memories weren't his, alone.

"Grake." He turned and saw T'Prylla. He extended one hand and they touched fingers with what, for Vulcans, amounted to deep passion.

"We haven't been apart," T'Prylla said, some confusion evident. "Yet we have been separated. Where are the children? And where are Anauk and T'Kosa?"

"I remember them. We were all together."

"Yet . . . not." They stood in the middle of the research dome, surrounded by jumbled mounds of reassembled equipment. The devices they had used to chart the birth of the protostars had been inactive for nine years, most of their parts scavenged and used to create the engineer's nightmare which filled the dome. "What is your last memory . . . your own memory?"

"Radak and T'Raus, together . . ." Grake hesitated. "Telling us we were not going to be hurt, just—"

"Adapted," T'Prylla finished. "And so we have been. How much time has passed? Why call us back?"

Grake gestured at the massed machinery. "We must destroy this—immediately!"

Radak appeared out of nothing in front of them. "Honored parents," he said. "It is necessary to return the station to normal operations."

"My son," Grake said. "What we have been doing is *maut akspra*. It must stop, now!" Grake held out his hand to Radak. The boy looked at his father's outstretched fingers, blinked slowly, then turned away. "Much has been accomplished," he said. "We are grateful to you. But we have guests now. Those that you summoned, ten years ago, have finally arrived."

"There is a ship?" T'Prylla asked.

"A large and well-armed ship," Radak said. "A group of humans appeared in the *reshek* corridor." The station's sections were named according to the symbols of the Vulcan alphabet, of which *reshek* was the third.

"Where are they?" T'Prylla asked.

"They returned before I could do more than greet them. Why were no Vulcans among them, Mother?"

T'Prylla approached her son—or the image of her son, she did not know which—and slowly reached for his shoulders with her hands. She grasped solid flesh, covered with perfectly tangible green cloth—the same children's uniform Radak had worn for a decade, but altered to fit his growing body. "There isn't much time," she said. "These are our rescuers. We sent them a distress signal. They will not leave until they have discovered what happened, and corrected the situation. Or until they have taken us all away."

Radak's eyes widened with alarm. "That would be horrible," he said. "We must stay."

"Why?" Grake asked.

"It is not for you to know, yet," Radak said.

"But they have seen you. They know we are here—"

"They have seen me, but they know nothing else. They do not know anybody else is alive on the station. We have masked everything, and we have not replied to their messages—"

"Why so devious?" Grake asked. "They are here for our good."

"Not so. The good is realized by our staying here, by continuing our work . . . not by leaving. We do not need to be rescued."

"Who are you?" T'Prylla asked suddenly. Radak focused his eyes on her coldly. There was no hint of affection, only a curious kind of heightened interest.

"I am your son," he said.

"Where is T'Raus?"

"She is involved in work. You must cooperate with us—"

"And the others?"

"They are well. They work with us, just as you have."

"We cannot cooperate," Grake said slowly, circling his son. The boy followed him from the corners of his eyes, his body betraying no sign of tension. "You hold us prisoner. You allow us no freedom, no true participation. You make us your slaves, and you tell us nothing. This cannot be tolerated. You are not behaving as a son should—"

"Because I have higher duties now," Radak said. "You do not choose to cooperate?"

"No," T'Prylla said. There was no use lying. They could hide nothing from this form of Radak, whatever he was.

"Then we have no choice but to adapt you again. There is no harm—"

Grake's arm shot out for his son's shoulder, fingers and thumb configured to pinch a sensitive nerve and render the boy unconscious. But Radak vanished even as the fingers closed. His voice whispered in the air around them. "I am sorry, my parents."

T'Prylla watched in horror as Grake's face grew rigid, then softened. All resistance vanished in her husband's features. Then her own will seemed to melt, and she was returned to the undifferentiated state in which they had both spent the past nine years. Deep inside, however—below all the carefully nurtured, civilized levels, in the regions of her personality that emulated the violent Vulcan figures of the past—T'Prylla hated, and fought, and screamed with rage . . .

"Mr. Veblen, I have to say I don't place much trust in your stochastic algorithm. Still, since nothing else seems to make much sense, what do the new versions tell us?" Kirk sat in his favorite chair, a worn manually-operated Delkin he had purchased while on shore leave some years before. On the cabin's more modern conference chairs sat Spock, Veblen, McCoy, Ensign Devereaux, Lieutenant Olaus and Mason, who carried a simple voice recorder.

"Sir," Veblen began, swallowing. "The computers suggest the algorithms are not appropriate at this point. We are close to having information we can use to find out what really happened—"

"Oh? How close are we?" Kirk turned to Spock. "Are the enhancements any help?"

"Whatever Ensign Devereaux saw in the station corridor, it does not register on the tricorder. And Mister Mason's opinion to the contrary, we are fortunate the tricorder was present, and not her own press equipment; the tricorder is far more diversified and sensitive."

"Mr. Devereaux?"

"The picture of the boy—he was only three years old at the time the record was made. I can't be positive. But it does resemble the older boy I saw in the station."

"Spock, any chance there would be other Vulcan children on the station by now?"

"Not of that age, Captain."

"Of course. So how does Radak become so disembodied that he doesn't show up on a tricorder?"

"There is only one way to find out, Captain. We must send down another landing party."

"Spock, I've been known to take risks, but I'm not sure that's one I want to take right now—"

Uhura's voice broke in over the com. "Captain, a signal from Station One has just come in."

Kirk sat up. "Relay, Lieutenant."

"With visual, Captain."

Kirk reached over and activated his cabin screen. The image was hazy at first, but quickly sharpened. Kirk recognized Grake immediately; the Vulcan looked tired, but sounded as enthusiastic as possible for a Vulcan. "This is researcher Grake on Black Box Nebula Station One. I wish to speak to the captain of the Federation starship *Enterprise*."

"I'm Captain James T. Kirk. We're relieved to see you alive and well, Grake. We've had some alarming moments in your station."

"Yes, my son informed me. I apologize for the confusion. We have been rather isolated here, and all of our communications equipment has been deactivated to transfer power to other projects. We are all indeed well, Captain—with the exception, unfortunately, of our colleagues in suspended animation."

"Tell him we have to come down soon," McCoy said.

"Request permission to enter your station and carry out our orders," Kirk said. "We are acting on your distress call, Grake."

"Yes, of course. It has been a very long time, Captain, even for Vulcans. Much has changed . . . and some of the changes may be startling. May I suggest that only essential personnel be sent down first?"

"Of course. Spock, myself and Dr. McCoy will be in the second landing party."

"Yes, how marvelous. T'Prylla and I will be very pleased to see Spock again. And of course, all of you have been long awaited."

Kirk glanced at Spock, who was out of range of the console cameras. His first officer's expression was troubled, verging on a frown. "Please give us proper coordinates, Grake," Kirk said, "so we won't interfere with any of your . . . ah . . . projects."

Grake read them transporter coordinates and repeated his gladness at seeing them, then signed off. "Spock?" Kirk asked when the screen had gone dark. "Something wrong?"

"I cannot be sure, Captain. I knew Grake only briefly, and that more than twenty years ago."

"And?"

"I must inspect the situation more closely before I voice any hypothesis," Spock said. His look said, in a way that Kirk was quite capable of interpreting, that a Vulcan could maintain a record for accurate observations only if not pressed at a premature moment.

"Very well. Thank you, Ensign, Mr. Olaus.

Rowena, you'll be allowed on the planetoid as soon as we decide it is safe. The second party will transport as soon as Dr. McCoy has assembled his equipment."

"I'll be ready in ten minutes, Captain," McCoy said. "I'll want Nurse Chapel with me."

"Fine." When he was alone in his quarters, Kirk played back the message and searched Grake's face closely, trying to find what Spock had found . . . something so vague and uncertain the Vulcan couldn't yet express it. Kirk sensed something, too . . .

Something very disturbing.

Chapter Eleven

McCoy was in a fever of activity. He ordered the nurses about sharply, efficiently, his southern drawl becoming so pronounced that occasionally he had to repeat his orders to be understood, which exasperated him no end. The TEREC analyzer—a box about a foot on each side—waited on its floating pallet as other medical supplies were added, including the TEREC remote probe, a diagnostics tricorder and McCoy's "little black bag," a customized general practice unit now equipped for the Vulcan inhabitants of Station One. Mason watched and recorded and did her best to stay out of his way, not that McCoy would have said a harsh word to her. Already, she felt a very father-daughter relationship blossoming between them, though few words had been said. She wondered if it was her gamine personality that attracted McCoy, but suspected it was her small-planet-girl handicap.

The pallet, full to overflowing, was rushed by a harried ensign to the elevator. McCoy followed,

Chapel in tow, as both donned pocket-studded medical field jackets. "He handles that pallet like it was a mule," McCoy undertoned, passing Mason. Mason grinned and fell in behind.

In the transporter room, Kirk and Spock were strapping on their security belts and phasers as McCoy and Chapel entered and positioned the pallet over its disk on the platform.

Shallert stood ready at the controls. When Kirk and Spock were in position, they were joined by Chekov, who doubled as part of Olaus's security team. Shallert switched on the transporter. McCoy muttered something beneath his breath until his eye caught Mason's, and he flashed a brave and utterly false smile.

"Let's go, Mr. Shallert," Kirk said. Shallert initiated beaming.

While in the transporter beam, there is no sensation of time or event. At the most, one feels a slight tickle at the base of the neck (Dr. McCoy cannot explain this, but the sensation is experienced at least once by anyone who has ever been transported.) Rumors of spiritual experiences, of the feeling that one has died and returned to life, or seen what lies beyond death—or even more pervasive rumors of those who have the talent to see the future while being transported—have never been substantiated. And yet . . .

Spock, the least likely to put any credence into such rumors, feels a touch, the merest feathery whisper of inquiry, as if the scattered particles that will reassemble as himself are being individually examined . . .

"Spock. Spock!"

They stood in the broad equipment storage dome of Station One, clustered around Spock, who lay flat on his back, not moving. Kirk bent over his first officer, while McCoy checked the Vulcan's pulse at his armpit. Spock's eyes fluttered and he turned his head. The first face he saw was that of Radak, watching him with curious interest from behind the larger forms of Grake and T'Prylla.

"Jim, I want that transporter torn apart top to bottom," McCoy said softly. "I've never liked that thing, and so help me, I'll shut it down—"

"Done. Spock, are you okay?"

"I do not seem to be injured," Spock said, getting to his feet with McCoy's help. The dome interior was empty, the flat gray aggregate flooring marked by pressure and skid marks where supplies had once rested.

Kirk flipped open his communicator and ordered a thorough maintenance check on the transporter.

"Am I the only one affected?" Spock asked.

"I'm fine," Chapel said, aiming the diagnostic tricorder at Spock's chest. Chekov agreed that he, too, felt no ill effects. Kirk turned to the group awaiting them.

"I apologize for a very clumsy arrival," he said. "But it appears to be a minor problem. I'd like to introduce the ship's doctor and his assistant, Dr. Leonard McCoy and Lieutenant Christine Chapel. I'm Captain James Kirk, this is Ensign Chekov, and this . . . as I'm sure you are aware," he said to T'Prylla, "is my first officer and the science officer of the *Enterprise*, Commander Spock."

"Welcome to the Black Box Nebula, Captain," T'Prylla said, extending her hand. Her grip on Kirk's hand was firm and dry, warmer even than Spock's. "If it is possible for the members of such a small team to welcome anyone to such a vast territory. My husband has already extended his appreciation, and I wish to reiterate. I am T'Prylla. This is our assistant astrophysicist, Anauk." The Vulcan male divided the fingers of one hand in the traditional greeting. "This is his clan-mate, T'Kosa. And our son, Radak, whom some of your crew have already met. Our daughter, T'Raus, is involved in a project at this time."

"Our first priority is to give all of you a thorough medical exam," McCoy said.

"That will not be necessary," Grake said, nodding

79

graciously at McCoy. "We have an excellent medical center here. I am afraid those who most need your help, are quite beyond it."

"If you're referring to the sleepers," McCoy said, "we may be able to save them. And as for your health, Starfleet regulations require that I make my own judgment."

"Dr. McCoy is right," Kirk said. "And while he and Nurse Chapel are doing that, I'd like to begin the de-briefing."

"Of course," T'Prylla said. "Anything we can do to oblige our rescuers. Though we must warn you, the situation is not nearly as desperate as it seemed when we issued our distress signal."

McCoy asked to be taken to their medical facilities. Grake led the way, and Kirk turned to Spock and Chekov. "I want you to keep an eye on Radak," he said when the others were out of hearing.

"Is there anything wrong with the boy?" Chekov asked, puzzled.

"He isn't a ghost. Just watch him."

"Yes, sir."

Kirk took a deep breath and motioned for Spock and Chekov to come along. Spock was interested in Kirk's tone of voice. As usual, Kirk was attuned to the same incongruities as his first officer, though he reacted quite differently—with an irritated, almost angry brusqueness. "Spock," he said. "I seem to recall that this dome was supposed to be full of emergency supplies."

"It is so described in the inventory of Station One," Spock said.

"Then where is all of it? Would they have used it all by now?"

"It is conceivable, Captain, though not if damage was as low as we're being led to believe."

They walked to the hatch leading out of the storage dome and into the *reshek* corridor. "What does your tricorder say about Radak?"

Spock held up the instrument and showed Kirk the readout. "He is a quite normal fifteen-year-old Vulcan boy. His data are very distinct."

Kirk nodded and increased his walking speed. Chekov broke into a short run to catch up.

The station medical center had been altered drastically. McCoy looked around in dismay at the barely concealed evidence of tampering, rebuilding of equipment, removal of furniture and diagnostic machines. "This place is a shambles," he said to Chapel. "What in God's name happened here?"

Grake stepped forward and removed an unfamiliar chromium sphere from a plain black metal box. "T'Kosa has made important advances. This is the only device we use for medical attention now. The rest of the equipment, wherever possible, has been converted to help us with our research."

He handed McCoy the chromium sphere. It weighed at most a pound, and had no visible surface features. "It is quite easy to use. I highly recommend it."

"How . . ." McCoy began.

"If there is a medical problem, the device diagnoses the problem and cures it upon request. It responds to Vulcan now, but it would only take a moment's effort to have it respond to Federation English."

"I'm more familiar with my own equipment," McCoy said. "Thanks, but I'll stick with that for the time being." He gestured at the pallet of medical supplies. "I'll examine the children first. Could you bring T'Raus in here? And while we're waiting for her . . ." He smiled and crooked a finger at Radak. The boy stepped forward and submitted to Chapel's quick pass of the diagnostic tricorder over him. Grake went to a wall-mounted com terminal and spoke a few words of Vulcan into it.

McCoy dug into the contents of his bag and

brought out the subcutane, loading it with a vial of nutrients and vitamins. Radak pulled away from Chapel as McCoy wielded the automatic syringe over the boy's arm. "No!" Radak protested. McCoy put on his most soothing expression.

"It's quite painless. Just a warm pressure—"

"My son is saying that supplements or any other medications are unnecessary."

"And I'm saying that it's my duty—"

"Never mind, Bones," Kirk said, entering the medical center. A step behind him was a slender young Vulcan girl, perhaps two years junior to Radak, walking hand-in-hand with Spock. Chekov maneuvered through the door around them.

"Jim, there are regulations I have to follow if we're going to interact with personnel—"

"I have T'Raus's guarantee that the staff of Station One is healthy."

McCoy regarded Kirk with pained confusion.

The girl, her straight and flawless black hair cut shoulder-length, let go of Spock's hand and stood beside T'Kosa. "We have done remarkable things here," the girl said, "and you may require a little time to get used to them. Until then, please do not force your regulations upon us. You may examine us, as you wish, but we are quite capable of treating ourselves."

McCoy recovered his decorum almost immediately. "Then, if I'm allowed, I'd better see to the people in cold storage. That is, unless I'm pre-empted there, too . . ."

"We do not object to your efforts," T'Kosa said. "For us, they have been dead ten years."

"That's what I was afraid you'd say," McCoy muttered. As T'Kosa made a move to come with McCoy and Chapel, the doctor stopped her by holding up his hand. "The captain needs you here more than I do. If nothing's been changed, we should do just fine by ourselves."

"Then we will begin formal debriefing right

away," T'Prylla said. "There is so much to tell, and so many records to show . . ."

Even as they gather in the room where meals are shared, T'Prylla struggles to find her own memory of the past ten years. She cannot control her speech or her actions but perhaps she can recall all that has happened, as she witnessed it . . .

But it is confused. There was the construction of the Transformer, completed without the aid of any of the adults, using equipment in the storage dome . . . And the memories of that are mixed, not hers alone. Although she does recall the wonder and terror of her realization that her own small children had accomplished something beyond the ability of the most brilliant Vulcan engineers. Will the rescuers be told of the Transformer? Or of the Eye-to-Stars?

McCoy and Chapel stood in the cylindrical cold room, wearing environment packs that projected a curtain of warmth around them. The helium atmosphere outside the shimmering curtains was a brisk −260° Celsius; the temperature within the hibernacula suspended around the chamber was only a few degrees above absolute zero.

McCoy had examined the freezing and revival equipment, and everything seemed to be in order. Chapel went from hibernaculum to hibernaculum, taking detailed tricorder readings. McCoy checked the last available medical records of the individuals suspended in the cold room and compared them with Chapel's findings. As he expected, the individuals had aged perhaps one hour in ten years . . . and yet all were clinically dead. The myelin sheathing on virtually all of their nerves had broken down under unprecedented levels of Ybakra radiation.

McCoy had a bizarre vision of what would happen if they were revived now . . .

The hibernacula would open on cue, and the people within would try to move. Each would experience a horrible, agonizing convulsion, but within seconds they would be isolated from their misery . . . and from life itself.

"I thought I had them licked, but those damned medical monitors are going to fight us every step of the way," McCoy said. "Or I'm back on the farm playing OB-GYN to the chickens." Chapel suppressed a smile by looking at the cold, frozen face of one of the thirty suspended team-members. "These people are technically dead, and I'm not going to be allowed to play God by bringing them back to life."

"Yes, but they're not physically dead," Chapel said. "Not yet . . ."

"Hell, they've been dead for ten years. Total nerve damage, through and through . . . that's one of the definitions of irreversible death fed into the monitors. It hardly matters that they're very well-preserved."

"But . . . *can* we save them? I mean, is it possible?"

McCoy shook his head. "Only if I play Clarence Darrow to a robot with a tin ear for rhetoric."

According to Grake, the station had been swept for months by intense and intermittent storms of radiation. The planetoid had been propelled a few degrees from its former position by fierce particle bombardment. Fortunately, the station had been in the planetoid's shadow for most of the violent buffeting, and they had spent the first two months in a shelter proofed against all harmful radiation but Ybakra. Sensors on the other side of the planetoid had fed the researchers the data they required to determine the position and spectral type of the new stars. Initially, there had been eighteen possible protostar clouds in their section of the nebula, but at least seven of them—those most likely to begin fusion—had been disrupted and destroyed by their precocious siblings.

"That was just as well," Grake said, though with

some hint of regret in his voice. "We could have used more data on other starbirths, but our time in the shelter was running out, and the particle bombardment would probably have killed us."

When the situation had stabilized and the stars had settled on their path to the main sequence, the researchers had emerged from the shelter to discover that their comrades in cold storage had been severely injured. "The hibernacula are heavily shielded against most forms of radiation," T'Kosa explained. "We were not prepared for so much Ybakra, and believed that proximity to the planetoid would keep levels down. There is no other way to shield against Ybakra . . . we could have done nothing more, anyway."

Spock intercepted Kirk's glance but said nothing, and Kirk likewise kept his counsel.

"We were able to repair most of the damage to the station, and to resume our work," Grake said. "We realized we could never use sub-space radio to communicate with the Federation, since in the presence of the mass anomalies the Ybakra would totally block all fraction-space transmissions, so I set about creating a very powerful tight-beam radio signal transmitter. I knew the location of a Federation buoy beyond the boundaries of the Black Box, but only approximately, since our position had been changed and our view of other stars was obscured by the expanding nebula gas clouds. Still, I was able to send the signal . . ."

Radak looked up from the table at Spock. "We assume the message was only partially intercepted."

"Yes," Spock said. "We received a fair amount of science data, but very little of Grake's audio-visual transmission."

"That, too, is for the best. We were pessimistic about our chances, and the message may have caused undue alarm. As it is, we have done quite well. And we have made significant advances in our understanding—not only about stellar processes, but about physics in general. We will soon be able to show you our new research center, perhaps after Dr. McCoy has finished with the sleepers."

"We may have problems rescuing your people quickly," Kirk said. "We were not prepared to take on such a large job. It could take weeks."

"There is also some doubt that the nebula has stabilized," Spock said. "We strongly recommend you all come aboard the *Enterprise,* and return with us to the nearest starbase as soon as we've transported the sleepers."

Radak shook his head once, firmly, and Grake did likewise. "That is impossible, Spock," T'Prylla said. "There can be no interruptions in our work. We do not require rescuing, as you can plainly see. And if the nebula should be agitated again . . . we have survived once. We are much more prepared now. You will better comprehend how safe we are when you've seen the research dome."

"Do not misunderstand," Radak said.

"We have been here, out of touch with everyone, doing our work," T'Prylla continued, as if on cue from her son. "To have fellow beings with us, to compare our findings with the work of other scientists—with what has been happening in the Federation in the last ten years—is marvelous." She looked at Spock with an expression that on a human face would have been interpreted as stern. Spock lifted an eyebrow and withdrew a data pack from his belt pouch.

"I anticipated such a need," he said, handing the pack to T'Prylla. "Here you will find all the research results published in your fields of interest. There has been considerable progress in understanding subspacial mass anomalies." He paused. "And there has been much change in the *Spyorna* on Vulcan."

T'Prylla did not react to Spock's last bit of information. She took the proferred pack and passed it to Grake. "In return, we have prepared a report on our protostar and Ybakra studies." *Severely edited*

. . . "How quickly can the sleepers be moved to the *Enterprise?*"

"For the moment, we can only beam up six at a time," Kirk said, "and reconstruct two a week. We're investigating rigging the shuttlecraft to ferry the hibernacula, but even that would take time and present some risks." And for that reason, he thought, we could certainly use a little more cooperation . . .

Chapter Twelve

The TEREC analyzer, at McCoy's request, sent its remote probe around the cold storage chamber for a second time before returning a final answer. McCoy and Chapel waited outside the cylindrical cold chamber, watching through the glass port as the probe floated from hibernaculum to hibernaculum, calculating the mass and complexity of each of the thirty frozen researchers. The remote probe acted as a scan-only transporter, with neither the power nor the equipment to actually disintegrate and reintegrate anything. It fed its results to the analyzer, which considered the situation and decided what the TEREC was capable of doing, practically and legally. McCoy had few doubts what the answer would be.

"Slow as molasses," he grumbled, pulling up a seat and squatting with the back pulled to his chest, legs straddled on either side. Chapel stood by the port, arms crossed, with her hands gripping her shoulders.

"Just looking in there makes me feel frozen," she said. "Ten years in cold storage . . ."

"Yes, and even without Ybakra, I don't think there's been such a prolonged freeze in a century. They were only supposed to be in there two or three years, until the preliminary work had been done by T'Prylla and her people."

"I wonder what it would be like to work with Vulcans . . . I mean, almost everybody being Vulcan but you." There were four humans in cold storage; all the rest were Vulcans.

"They were volunteers. I suppose they knew what they were getting into. From what Spock says, T'Prylla isn't exactly your straight-forward Vulcan. She's even odder than Spock, not that you'd notice."

"Analysis completed," said the analyzer.

"Well, let's have it," McCoy urged impatiently.

"These individuals have all suffered severe nerve damage in cold storage. They are legally dead. The TEREC unit is forbidden by its monitors from reviving beings who are dead by the definition established for each category of being."

"Damn," McCoy said.

"There would be practical difficulties, as well. Since the bodies can only be transported once, without suffering even more severe damage due to the dangers of transporting deep-frozen specimens, and since therefore they must be fed directly into the TEREC, only six may be transported at a time. The TEREC can hold two form-memories for restructuring, and four in auxiliary banks."

"Yes, yes, we knew all that. If we have to, we can bring them all up on the shuttle . . . though Scotty alone knows how we'll rig the power supplies and safeguards. Show me a profile on the typical case for Vulcans and humans." The analyzer displayed a multi-dimensional chart in three separations, giving the scanning results for a Vulcan and a human. The doctor stared at the results for a moment, repeated the display, and frowned. "Something isn't right here. The bodies have been tampered with, or I'm greatly mistaken. But that doesn't make sense. Maybe the probe needs adjusting." McCoy shut off the analyzer and rested his chin on his crossed wrists.

In the station mess, Kirk was not encouraged by McCoy's expression when the doctor and Chapel returned.

"If the transporters are working properly, we can move up the first six patients now. The rest we may be able to transport in the shuttle. Either way, it'll take us fifteen weeks to reconstruct the people in cold storage. The major problem is whether we can work our way around the monitors."

"They're going to block it?" Kirk asked.

McCoy pursed his lips and lifted his hand. "Hold on a minute. We're not out yet, just down. We have to return to the ship and discuss strategy. Since these people are all in prime physical condition and don't seem to need us right away, I presume that's allowed?"

"We have completed our first de-briefing," Spock said. "I believe it would be useful to return to the *Enterprise*. We can be replaced by a security team."

Radak protested. "We have no need for protection."

"It's part of the regulations," Kirk said. The boy irritated him. "Station One is now in extended status. There has to be a team in the station at all times." He flipped open his communicator. "Kirk to *Enterprise*."

"*Enterprise*, Uhura here, Captain."

"How does the transporter check out?"

Uhura brought Scott on the line. "Captain, there's not a thing wrong with it. It's in prime condition."

"Any explanation for what happened to Mr. Spock?"

"No, sir. But I cannot blame the machines. My crews have been over them four times."

90

"Will he guarantee my atoms won't be spread over known space?" McCoy asked.

"Aye, Doctor," Scott said. "That I will, or throw out my engineering degrees and become a brewmaster."

"Not a fair exchange," McCoy said under his breath.

"We'll need a security team to replace us. Transport all of us but Chekov, and send down two replacements for the next watch period. Kirk out." He turned to Chekov. "Brief your replacements and stay with them until the change of watch. Then I want you back within four hours."

"Yes, sir."

Spock, Kirk, McCoy and Chapel began to transport seconds later. When they were gone, Chekov smiled nervously at the Vulcans and stood stiffly by the door of the mess. "I hope the presence of my men won't inhibit you," he said.

"They are most welcome," Radak said, passing him to leave. Grake, T'Prylla and T'Kosa followed. Anauk ordered Vulcan food from the autochef, then followed his comrades out the door to eat in privacy.

"I'm sure we all have questions," Kirk said as they stepped down from the transporter stage.

"And I'm sure you know what my question is," McCoy said, guiding the medical pallet.

"In my quarters. We need to talk. Let our hair down." He looked at Spock. "Most of us, anyway."

McCoy left the pallet in Chapel's charge and followed Kirk and Spock to the elevator. Just as the doors closed, two ensigns began beaming down to the station.

Kirk walked through the doors to his cabin and ran his hands through his hair. "God help us," he said. "There's something—"

"Why did you usurp my authority as ship's doctor?" McCoy asked sharply, confronting him.

"Because they were clearly reluctant to be treat-ed," Kirk said. "And T'Raus hinted they would refuse if the issue was pressed. Regulations are regulations, Bones, but can we actually force them to submit?"

McCoy backed off, hands on hips. He had no immediate answer, but his anger still hadn't subsided.

"Spock, why shouldn't we tell them about Ybakra shields?" Kirk asked.

"I cannot answer that question at the moment, Jim. But there is something clearly amiss on Station One, and we should come to grips with it right away."

"I'll tell you one thing that's wrong," McCoy said. "The TEREC analyzer picked up some anomalous data. It had no immediate bearing on the case, but it doesn't make sense."

"And what's that?"

"Jim, the people in cold storage have been interfered with. I couldn't figure out the analyzer displays until a few minutes ago, but I'd swear something has been *tapping* them, drawing information from their brains, or storing information there. Now while we're talking about regulations, may I point out how illegal that is?"

"Jim," Spock said, "T'Prylla evinced not the slightest interest when I mentioned that the *Spyorna* had undergone change. That is not characteristic. Nor, I must say, is the behavior of their son and daughter. A Vulcan youth is not allowed to guide the conversation of his elders, certainly not past the age of *ka nifoor*."

"So what does it all add up to?"

"There's trouble in River City," McCoy said.

"I beg your pardon, Doctor?" Spock said, genuinely puzzled.

"Never mind. Jim, we should clear them all out and comb that station centimeter by centimeter. I don't trust any of them."

"For once, Doctor, we are in agreement," Spock said. "Though I am reluctant to detail all of my misgivings, there is something definitely wrong on Station One."

"Okay, we're agreed on that. Now for the next problem. The monitors aren't going to let us revive the sleepers."

"That just confirms our worst fears," Kirk said.

"Yes, and I'm not totally unprepared. I'm going to go up against the monitors. I'm going to fool them, Jim, and to do that, I'll need—"

"Bones—"

"I'll need both of you to help me."

"Bones, if we mess with the monitors, it means my command. Worse, it means all of us will face court-martial."

"They sent us here to rescue the people on Station One, and we can't do it because of a prissy computer with prissy laws built in! My job is to save lives, Jim, whether regulations allow it or not!"

"Clearly, technology has outstripped Federation laws," Spock said. "I, too, have investigated the possibility of failings within the monitors."

McCoy stared goggle-eyed at Spock, then smiled. "By God," he said. "I'm beginning to like this tall green–blooded fellow."

Kirk sat down heavily on his couch and laid both palms on the low table before him. "It would take two weeks for a subspace message to go out to Starfleet and come back. I've taken risks in my career, and I've stretched the regulations often enough that you should know I'm not squeamish. But I do worse than disobey Starfleet if we circumvent the monitors. I disobey my oath to serve the Federation. Every one of us owes our allegiance to the Federation, the civilian branches of government."

"Jim, I don't ask that we shut the monitors down. Only that we tickle them a bit."

"And how do you suggest we do that, Doctor?" Spock asked.

Kirk glanced between them. "I never thought I'd see the day when you two would be in cahoots."

"Why, Spock, seeing that you're so sympathetic, I was hoping you might be able to suggest something."

Chapter Thirteen

Mason stepped up to the door of the computer control center and braced herself. The door opened, and she was vastly relieved to find Veblen inside; Spock was not present. "The captain says I can find all the debriefing materials in the open log."

Veblen looked at her blankly, then leaned his head back and opened his mouth in an O. "You can access the open log through your quarters terminal. You don't have to come down here."

"I do," she said, "if I want to find out what's really going on. Is there anything not being put in the open log?"

Veblen smiled and shook his head. "I'm not the one to ask, Miss Mason."

She sat down in the console chair across from him and sighed deeply. "Thank God for someone who's willing to call me Miss instead of Mister. The captain did it once, but I'm sure he was being tactical. Why shouldn't I ask you?"

Veblen looked away, still smiling. "No comment to the press. But it should be obvious."

"I shouldn't come to you just because you're the odd man out, that's what you're saying?"

He nodded. "It's only natural. I bring the bad news. Since I'm staff instead of line, I don't get to do much else *but* bring bad news. And the bad news this time is in the open log; the captain put it there himself."

"Save me the trouble. I have to file a dispatch soon and I can't afford the luxury of deep research."

"The monitors are refusing to revive the frozen station personnel."

"In God's name, why?"

"Because they are legally dead."

"That's nonsense. If they can be revived, they aren't dead!"

"I only bring the news, I don't justify it."

Mason leaned forward. "Are the monitors questioning Kirk's ability to command?"

This took Veblen aback. "Not at all," he said. "The captain has satisfied the monitors completely."

"And Dr. McCoy?"

"Dr. McCoy hasn't done anything but ask the monitors to make a judgment."

"There's no possibility Dr. McCoy is doing something wrong, and the monitors are balking because of that?"

"No possibility at all," Veblen said. He finished typing a series of commands into his console and pushed his chair back. "I think we should go . . . what's the phrase . . . off the record now."

"Certainly," Mason said.

The door opened and Spock entered. Mason sat straight up in the chair and avoided Spock's eyes. "Thank you, Mr. Veblen," she said, her voice higher pitched than before. "We'll talk later."

After she had left, Veblen prepared the screen for Spock's file work. "I don't think she's used to you, Mr. Spock," Veblen said.

Spock did not react. "Mr. Veblen, Dr. McCoy

requests a list of the monitors' medical reference files."

"Yes, sir. I've finished processing the station data on Ybakra. As soon as I've made a hard copy for the doctor, I'll take a rest, unless you have further need of me."

"Thank you, Mr. Veblen, no."

Veblen caught up with Mason at a crew reference terminal outside the non-commissioned officers' lounge. "Could we talk for a moment?" he asked.

"Off the record, or on?"

"Off. About you, and about what I said just a few minutes ago."

"Sure." They took the elevator to Area 39, the all-crew recreation room, and found a seat at an empty games table in an isolated corner.

"First," Veblen said, "I don't appreciate your coming to me as if I were the weak point in the *Enterprise* crew."

"That wasn't my intention at all—"

"Second, I think you're on the wrong track, and I think you have some problems of your own to solve."

"Where do you get off—"

"Wait a minute. You said you'd hear me out." He stared at her with an intensity which cut off any further protest. "I'll tell you why I'm angry all of a sudden. Sure, I wear my uniforms a little out of regulation, and I'm not in the best shape compared to the rest of the crew. And I'm staff, the only staff officer aboard this ship. But I am no weak point, and my work proceeds no matter what anyone else's attitude to me is."

"It wasn't my intention—I mean, I've never thought of you as a weak point."

"Good. Then maybe my next shot will be more on target. I'm in charge of maintaining and testing the monitors. Incidentally, I work with Mr. Spock on all the ship's computers, because the monitors interface

97

with virtually every system on the *Enterprise*. And I work with the captain because the monitors are very complex, and no command officer should be expected to be completely familiar with such a new and difficult system."

"Yes," Mason said, watching Veblen closely.

"If you think there's a story in the captain's problems adjusting to the monitors, that's fine. We may be uncomfortable with that kind of coverage, but that's the way things are; it's a legitimate story. But if you think you're going to find material proving that Captain Kirk is trying to frustrate the monitors, to somehow get around them, I'm here to tell you that's a dead end. I've had the captain question me, even harangue me, about some point or other, but not once has he suggested I was at fault, or that I am not a part of the *Enterprise*. Any alienation you see is largely due to me, not to the captain or the crew."

"I have to follow my instincts, Mr. Veblen."

"We're in a very tough situation here. Even tougher than you know." Veblen looked down at the table. "I'm sorry if I've been angry with you. What I say next has to be doubly confidential . . ."

To Mason, it was obvious that despite everything he had just said, Veblen needed to let his hair down with someone. "We've been off the record. I keep my word."

"The monitors—aren't perfect. They're only as good as the people who programmed them, and the laws they follow are not perfect. Dr. McCoy is up against a brick wall. I'm not going to say why, just yet, but I want you to understand. I want *somebody* to understand. They're going to have to do something, and if worse comes to worse, they're going to have to find a way around the monitors. And I am going to have to oppose them. I don't want to, but I will."

Mason regarded him with new understanding and respect. Veblen was deeply troubled; Why, she thought, he's probably as enamored of Captain Kirk as the rest of the crew!

"So maybe that's where your story should be. If the Federation wants to keep track of every little thing a starship does, perhaps we should find ways to monitor those who make the laws and expect us to carry them out. It should work both ways."

"What's the doctor going to do?"

"I don't know. I don't want to know. What I don't know won't hurt me, right?"

She nodded. "So we're both outcasts here," she said. "By occupation, if nothing else."

"I hope you'll excuse me," Veblen said, flushing now. "But I believe you're having some problems, too."

"Oh?"

"Yes. I believe you're having difficulty facing up to Mr. Spock, perhaps even to Mr. Yimasa."

"What gives you that impression?" It was Mason's turn to redden.

"When I joined Starfleet, I came from an all-human enclave on Titan."

"Where's that?"

"Saturn's largest moon. My folks were among the terraformers. They were great people, but they fed me a lot of nonsense about Vulcans and Andorrans and all the others—not those who don't have human shape; we hadn't even met any—but humanoids. I had a lot of garbage in my head to overcome. From the way you avoid Mr. Spock, and—" He paused. "Well, I've read parts of the file FNS sent up from Yalbo."

"My file?"

He nodded. "I think you have some of the same garbage to throw out. If it proves to be a problem, perhaps I can help."

"Thank you for the offer," Mason said, standing. "And I hope I've helped by being a sounding board."

Veblen shrugged.

"But from here on in, I think I'll want our interviews on the record. I have to get down to the station. I can't file reports when I haven't even been on the scene." She nodded curtly at him and left Area 39.

Chekov briefed his replacements, ensigns Pauli and Wah Ching, then called the *Enterprise* to be beamed back on board. As the transporter effect began, he saw Radak watching from the storage dome hatch. Parallel red lines crossed his vision as the beam disassembled his visual cortex; there was nothing unusual in that. But the expected reverse effect, and the appearance of the transporter room on the *Enterprise,* did not follow. Instead, Ensign Pavel Chekov found himself in a very dark, very lonely place, filled with a multitude of precisely phrased questions . . .

"Transporter interrupt!" Shallert punched the engineering alert button and immediately brought the backup systems on line. The transporter hummed a deep bass tone, which began to rise in frequency until it was a sweet, high whistle. Then the bass tone repeated.

"What is it, Mr. Shallert?" Scotty asked from the main engineering control deck.

"There's a delay in Ensign Chekov's assembly," Shallert said. "I have the backups—"

"Is he in form memory?" Scotty asked.

"I don't know, sir. The transporter isn't reporting anything."

"I'm on my way."

Just as Scott left the com, a single transporter effect began on the assigned disk. Shallert watched in amazement as Ensign Chekov assembled on the transporter deck—precisely forty seconds after he had been disintegrated on Station One.

* * *

"There's nothing wrong with the equipment," Scott repeated. He stood between McCoy and Kirk in the transporter room, his short black hair hanging in strands across his forehead, his uniform smudged and his hands clutching a pair of engineering diagnostic tricorders.

"Well, until you find out what *is* wrong," McCoy said, "I'm decertifying that monster." Scott turned to Kirk, his face betraying the most extreme anguish.

"Sir, if there had been ennathin wrong, Chekov wouldna' ha' come back at all!"

"Scotty, there was a delay. He wasn't beaming through solid steel, he was coming up through vacuum. There has to be some explanation. I believe the transporter is operating correctly, but I must go along with Dr. McCoy. Until we find out what caused the anomalies, we will take the shuttle and avoid transporting personnel."

Scotty agreed with a nod, but his shoulders slumped. "I'll take enna suggestions you have, gentlemen."

Chekov surveyed his quarters with wide-eyed interest. He picked up the glass artifact he had purchased from an Andorran crewmember two years before; it scintillated in his hands, appearing as spiky as a sea-urchin, but feeling like a smooth sphere to the touch. "Glass with the same index of refraction as air," he said to himself, in his own voice, though he did not do the talking. He turned to the screen and touched the keyboard beneath hesitantly.

"Perhaps I should speak to the ceptain," he said. "This does not feel right. I should not feel like this." He forced himself to reach out to the wall com, but his hand slowly withdrew before touching the button. Sweat broke out on his forehead. "I only wish to be left alone, and to feel well," he said. The presence interfering with his actions, and using his voice, did not respond.

Mason finished composing her dispatch and handed the data pack to Uhura on the bridge. Uhura plugged it into her console and asked, "Are we making the grade?"

"It's a very tame report, if that's what you mean," Mason said. "I can't get close enough to the action."

Kirk and Spock came on the bridge. "Rowena, we're taking a shuttle to the station," Kirk said. She stared at him expectantly.

"Dr. McCoy doesn't like the idea, but you're invited."

"I'll go," she said firmly. "I'll go, and thank you."

Chapter Fourteen

Very early in his life, McCoy had learned to disguise his deepest emotions. He had reached the conclusion that most other people did not feel as he did, or hid themselves even more effectively; either way, it was best not to demonstrate the extremes he often felt. The best disguise, he had discovered, was camouflage—hence, the brusque exterior he showed to even his oldest friends.

He was deeply romantic, even chivalrous, constantly feeling the urge to protect the "fair sex"; yet one couldn't treat female co-workers with such deference. The solution? Be brusque. And when his passionate respect for all living things became too painful to bear, he even hid from himself. In centuries past, he knew, he probably would have become an alcoholic; the stresses and strains would have produced an unbearable hormonal mix, and he would have turned to drink. Now, by tightly controlling his diet, taking adjustment drugs and engaging in various meditative therapies, he managed to keep the most destructive parts of himself under control.

He ragged Spock so unmercifully because he found himself dismayingly similar to the Vulcan.

McCoy's colleagues and friends—and one was very seldom not the other—soon came to accept the contradictions, and intuit the reasons behind them. They did not tender advice; it would have been useless. And, as Kirk well knew, however distressing McCoy's characteristics were to himself, they resulted in a damned fine doctor. What McCoy lacked in heady brilliance, he more than made up for in insight and compassion.

Even Spock respected the doctor's courtly bedside manner, since it was so effective, and not just on his human patients. Spock well remembered the healing of the silicon-based Horta, years before, accomplished by tenderness and the application of methods better suited to the building trades than formal medicine.

Now, McCoy faced a dilemma which put more than usual strain upon him. He had thirty patients which he had the technical means to save from living death, and yet he was being prevented from doing so. To circumvent those barriers, he had already hinted to Kirk, one of his finest friends, that they would have to bend or break the law. ("Shatter" would probably describe it best.) For Kirk to do so could mean the end of his career. And of course, it could mean the end of McCoy's career as well.

While McCoy focused on this problem, he could not avoid the other problems they were facing: the erratic functioning of the transporter, the peculiar situation on Station One, and the presence of a civilian journalist ready and waiting to record it all for public posterity.

McCoy sat in the shadowy darkness of his quarters, making notes on a piece of paper with an antique fountain pen beneath the concentrated beam of a small lamp. "With the transporter decommissioned until further testing, all the patients on Station One will have to be ferried to the *Enterprise* by shuttle. The shuttle is being outfitted for this job right now, but I'm not happy with the arrangements. Moving people in cold storage is risky business. The usual vibrations associated with travel in a small vehicle could be hazardous to those in deep cold. Even with special field suspension on each hibernaculum, there's risk. And rigging the shuttle with the special equipment means we can only carry two hibernacula at a time. Spock says the conditions in the nebula cloud are not ideal for small craft; the shuttle can't produce as strong a shield against radiation as the *Enterprise* . . ."

He rubbed his face with both hands and decided to put off his worries about the transfer. "How to get around the monitors . . ." He began his list of choices, none of which he was sure would work. "I've been considering some crazy scheme to rig a false message from the Federation, conveying new rule changes . . . a new definition of death. To that end, I've had a hard copy made of all the medical references in the monitors. But I'm certain Jim would veto any such scheme. And if Veblen found out about it . . . not good form to antagonize shipmates. Similar objections to finding a way to temporarily deactivate the medical monitoring functions. But now Spock—"

He lifted his fountain pen and stared off at a hologram of the salt marshes of Chincoteague Island. "Good old Spock," he resumed. "Spock has been laying hints all around about a way to get even deeper into the monitors, legitimately. The command monitors contain the experience-memories of six command-rank Starfleet officers. And in the medical monitors, there are six more—all ship's doctors . . ."

What was Spock's motivation in passing clues to McCoy? The doctor knew the answer immediately. As a Vulcan, Spock was primarily obedient to his duty, then to his commander, then to the mission. Spock's motivation was to eliminate a dilemma which could wreck not only their mission, but his commanding officer as well. Vulcan duty required no great respect for laws, especially human laws, that were self-defeating.

Trust a Vulcan to find a legitimate way to get around human inadequacies.

McCoy smiled. If all else failed, Spock would arrange for him to have a direct dialogue with the experience-memories in the medical monitors. There were no guarantees . . .

"But it's smarter to avoid taking the bull by the horns, when you can lead him around by the tail."

He put the paper away in his loose-leaf diary and screwed the pen back into its cap. Before he could proceed with Spock's help, he had to make sure they had the means to shuttle the hibernacula in the first place. He had long since learned to tackle problem in order of increasing difficulty; that way, if an problem was insoluble, no time was wasted on th next, tougher step.

Chekov jack-knifed abruptly in his bed and stared around the cabin, wide-eyed as if from some nightmare. Then, slowly, his eyes narrowed and he sank back onto the pillow. "Time," he requested.

"1207 hours," the console replied. In twenty minutes, he would be returning to the planetoid on the shuttle. He had slept very poorly, trying to resist the growing insanity—or so he interpreted the feelings of loss of will and unmotivated activity. He had tried to resist going to the console and doing what the new Voice requested, and had so far succeeded. But now it was too insistent. He knew he would stand up—

—He stood.

And go to the console.

—He went to the console.

He would call up a chart with the interior of the *Enterprise* laid out in graphic detail.

—He typed on the keyboard, trying to make mistakes and failing.

He would ask questions of the library computer—questions pertaining to specific details of the ship's engines, the matter-antimatter drives, with which he was not familiar.

—He typed more instructions. He made a hard copy of all the information he had called up. He inserted the copy card into his pouch. Then he went to the lavatory and made himself look presentable, ready for duty, though he could not eliminate the shadows around his eyes.

Thank you, said the Voice.

You are not in the least welcome, Chekov replied.

Chekov smiled and held out his arm, ushering Mason into the interior of the shuttle. Kirk and Spock were already inside, along with Chapel and McCoy. McCoy was carefully inspecting all the equipment newly installed to ferry the hibernacula. Chapel checked off items on her notepad as McCoy ran through all the crucial points. He stood up, pushing on his knees with his hands, and nodded to Kirk. "They're as good as they'll ever be," he said. "Who's going planetside with us?"

"Spock and presumably Rowena," Kirk said.

"I'd like to stay down there and file my reports from the station," Mason said.

"We'll need as much room as we can get on the return trip," McCoy said. "I'd like to bring up two hibernacula each trip."

Kirk looked around the group, then nodded. "Prepare for shuttle launch," he said. They took their seats—which had been rearranged around the area the hibernacula would occupy—and strapped themselves in. Mason turned around to watch the shuttle cargo doors being sealed, then attached the recorder to an equipment grip overhead, making sure the visual scanner could see out her port.

Chekov, seated next to her, observed closely but said nothing.

Outside the shuttle walls, the roar of air being evacuated from the shuttle hangar gradually reduced to a whisper, then a faint hiss. The deep grumble of the hangar doors opening was communicated to the shuttle through its landing supports, and ceased abruptly as the shuttle lifted off.

They exited the hangar on a reverse tractor beam, then switched on the impulse engines and descended to the planetoid.

T'Raus and T'Prylla dematerialized and crossed the space between the station and the Eye-to-Stars. It felt a bit like flying; unlike the transporter beam, their particular form of travel involved sensation and memory. T'Prylla enjoyed the journey much less than T'Raus; she could never quite be sure where they were going, or what would happen when they arrived.

The Voice she had heard so often inside her head—associated with the outburst of Ybakra from the triple stars—was familiar enough for her to give it a name: *Pau*, or in Federation English, "Corona." Corona never explained; all she had learned in the past nine years, she had deduced. She suspected her children were more privy to Corona's secrets.

They stood on the airless surface of the planetoid without suits, surrounded by a faint green envelope. T'Raus stretched out her hand and touched a meteoroid-scarred rock. Overhead, the constant purple glow of the nebula—very bright on the night side of the planetoid—seemed to bubble and distort. Gradually the distortion became perfectly round, and the Eye-to-Stars opened like a great black disk. T'Raus smiled and clapped her hands once. T'Prylla held out the astronomy tricorder, as she was willed to do, and let it record what the Eye-to-Stars saw.

When they were done—when the curiosity of Corona had been satisfied—T'Raus took the tricorder and played its information back. "This is very fine," she said. "Soon the work will be done." Then she frowned. "We cannot return to the precise position from which we left. There are more visitors. It is very *orniaga*."

T'Prylla had to think hard to remember what the Vulcan word T'Raus had used meant. It meant "irritated." She hadn't heard the word for decades; it was virtually never used in polite Vulcan conversation. She said nothing; she had no power to say anything. Her opinion was not wanted; only her scientific abilities, and her labor.

Her arm itched abominably, and she could not even scratch it . . .

Chapter Fifteen

The shuttle landed at the cargo lock of the storage dome, its landing fields disturbing years of micrometeoroid dust and ejecting it in straight rays from the pad. A boarding tube automatically stretched from the lock to the shuttle's rear cargo doors and connected with a sigh of equalizing pressures. Mason's ears popped. She reached up to release the recorder.

As the *Enterprise* party left the storage dome, Chekov broke away from the main group and encountered T'Raus in a side corridor near the research dome. Part of Chekov stared curiously at the closed hatches. No one had yet seen the station's rebuilt science areas. T'Raus held out her hand, and he gave her the hard copy of the *Enterprise* charts and specifications. She nodded, and without a word exchanged, he hurried to catch up with his shipmates before his absence was noticed.

The group passed by Wah Ching and Pauli, standing the current watch. Chekov relieved them and told them to return to the shuttle and wait for the rest of the group to join them. "Nothing to report?"

he asked, wondering if they, too, were being controlled. The burst of hidden anguish he felt was so intense that tears came to his eyes.

"Nothing unusual," said Pauli. "It's a bit chilly down here, society-wise, but I suppose that's not unusual." He grinned. The understood words were, "for Vulcans." Chekov watched them return to the storage dome.

McCoy and Spock went to the hibernaculum chamber, escorted by Anauk and T'Kosa. They turned on their environment fields and entered the chamber lock. The lock doors closed behind them, and they stood in the cold and silence. Outside, T'Kosa and Anauk waited to take them to the medical center for the scheduled meeting with Grake and T'Prylla.

Spock scanned the hibernacula with his science tricorder while McCoy took final measurements. The doctor bent down beside the hibernaculum closest to the inner chamber lock door and examined the connections on the power supply cables. "We'll have to move them quickly," he said. "The pallets can keep them cold for about five minutes. Then we'll hook them to the shuttle power supply."

Spock motioned for McCoy to examine the display on the science tricorder. "Your suspicions are correct," Spock said. "There is no further damage, but they have been tampered with."

"Why? What would the others gain?"

"As you suspected, the sleepers seem to have been utilized for information storage."

"That seems highly irregular, Spock. Besides, they're too cold for their brains to have any chemical activity."

"At their current temperature, their brains would have superconducting properties. No chemical activity would be needed; they could store enormous amounts of information without benefit of normal memory operations."

111

"If that's the case, thawing them would destroy the information . . . erase it."

Spock nodded.

"So what do you think the others will say?"

"If we are finished here, we can only go to the medical center and find out."

"Spock, you've been tight-lipped since before we arrived. You behave like a cat who knows where a whole cageful of canaries is hidden. Sometimes I get the willies just looking at you."

"I would assume that is a normal state of affairs, Doctor."

McCoy handed the tricorder back to him and shook his head. "Jim thinks we're conspiring on something. Maybe we are. If so, don't you think co-conspirators should share all their secrets?"

"Perhaps later," Spock said. McCoy knew better than to press him any further. They exited the cold lock and accompanied T'Kosa and Anauk to the meeting.

"We cannot allow removal of the sleepers," Grake said. He stood before the *Enterprise* visitors in the station medical center, hands gripping the edge of a stripped-down diagnostics table. "There is too much risk." T'Prylla, the children, T'Kosa and Anauk regarded the visitors with a calm isolation which, to Kirk, seemed like contempt.

"I've evaluated the risk," McCoy said. "There is some, but it's minimal." Kirk glanced at Spock to gauge his reaction to this turn of events. Spock stared intently at Grake, who refused to meet the first officer's eyes.

"While we respect Dr. McCoy's expertise, we have learned much about Ybakra radiation in the past ten years. We are constantly bathed in it, but at a level which cannot cause any more damage to the sleepers. The Ybakra is considerably reduced by proximity to our planetoid. In the shuttle, however, that protection is taken away. More damage may result."

McCoy stood and pointed a finger at Grake. "Your sleepers are as good as dead now. What can you do for them here?"

"We can protect them until a way is found to transport them to the *Enterprise* safely. Or until we devise a means of treating them ourselves."

"The *Enterprise* can't stay here indefinitely," Kirk said. "Frankly, I'm puzzled by the level of resistance we've met here. We are your rescuers, not your enemies." His voice was level, ominously so. "I stand by Dr. McCoy's decision to move the sleepers to the sickbay of the *Enterprise*."

T'Kosa stepped close to Grake. "I believe it is time we convince our visitors of how well we have done here, without their help."

Grake nodded. "There have been many delays, Captain, but now would seem to be a very appropriate time to show you the research dome."

"We're avoiding the issue," McCoy said, exasperated. "Jim, we're wasting time if we don't move the sleepers and begin reconstruction now!"

Kirk felt at a loss what to do. It was obvious that Spock still did not wish to reveal the existence of Ybakra shields, but mention of the technique now would save a great deal of trouble and argument. (Or would it? Would they find another excuse? And why didn't they know about Ybakra shields themselves? Their research on Ybakra had been comprehensive . . .) He disliked making decisions which would further antagonize McCoy, but he couldn't think of a way around it. "I think there's time enough to take a brief tour before we make our decision." He hoped McCoy could sense what was going on. The doctor looked even more exasperated, but did not protest further.

"Good," Grake said. "As I said before, I believe we have many surprises in store for you . . ."

* * *

Veblen finished checking the form-memory and experience-memory units of the transporter and shook his head. Scott waited anxiously a step behind him.

"I have to agree," Veblen said. "There's nothing wrong with the circuitry."

"Then it must be outside interference. Perhaps the radiation . . . ?"

"Ybakra operates in a different layer of fraction space than the transient memories," Veblen said, frowning. He took a data pack from his belt and hefted it, thinking. He had neglected to feed the new information from the station's researches on Ybakra radiation into the stochastic algorithm. "I don't think it would have any effect. However . . ."

"I'm at my wit's end," Scott said. "I've checked every aspect of transporter functioning, from power supplies to the memory coordinators. There is nothing wrong with the transporters." He put on a look of defiance. "It is not my machinery that's at fault! And I've never heard of a *delay* in transporter assembly."

"It's a puzzle," Veblen admitted. "I'll back your report as much as my expertise allows."

"Thank you," Scott said, relieved. Veblen left the transporter room and took the turbolift to the computer command center. He plugged the new information into the algorithm—which had been placed on temporary hold—and then asked for a specific level of inquiry. *Is there any chance,* he typed on the console, *that personnel aboard the station have learned to manipulate Ybakra, and are using that knowledge to cause anomalous events aboard the* Enterprise? He restarted the algorithm and leaned back in his chair, biting a fingernail and waiting for any coherent result.

Mason tugged the recorder closer to her and walked behind Radak. She felt completely out of place, and yet she had a strong sensation of something very important about to happen. Grake led the way to the research chambers, followed by T'Prylla and Spock. The others squeezed through the open hatchway after them, and all stood in a loose grouping to one side of the station's largest dome.

It was easy to see now where all the equipment in storage had been put to use. The dome was crowded with every conceivable combination of hardware, electronics and computers jury-rigged together in large piles, without much apparent regard for placement or visual order. To Mason, it looked like a child's playroom—a Vulcan child's playroom, perhaps, the child having been given anything he wished for. She glanced at Radak and T'Raus and met the girl's eyes. For a moment they stared directly at each other. Mason shuddered—and not just because the girl was Vulcan. She thought she was getting used to being around Vulcans. For all his quirks and strange appearance, Spock was certainly no ogre. But T'Raus . . .

There was a cold appraisal in her eyes that went beyond the constrained emotions of a Vulcan.

"Very impressive," Kirk said diplomatically. Grake walked them around the perimeter of the dome until they came to a raised platform, on which was mounted a small control panel. The FNS recorder positioned itself near the edge of the platform, motors within whining softly as its lenses followed Grake up the steps.

"It is a preliminary construction," Grake said, motioning for T'Prylla to join him. Radak followed his mother. "But what it does is much more impressive than its appearance suggests." Radak stood at the control panel. Grake seemed to hesitate before continuing his explanation. "With the Transformer, we are in control of all forms of matter, energy, space and time within the vicinity of the station. Our researches have given us mastery of the very founda-

115

tion of the universe, from which all creation arose. Our work is tentative, but we have accomplished a great deal."

Mason saw McCoy's lips move. He seemed to be saying something about madness.

"My son will prepare a demonstration."

Radak reached out to the dimly lighted switches on the panel and touched a few with the conservative grace born of long experience. *He knows the system better than his father,* Mason thought, wondering why Grake himself didn't perform the demonstration. The machinery in the dome made itself felt with a sensation beneath sound, a reminder of the presence of great power.

Then, very slowly, Radak faded. It took the visitors some seconds to realize what was happening. Chekov, even tightly controlled, jumped in startlement as the boy simply vanished. Mason believed she saw a flicker in the spot where the boy had stood, but it could have been a trick of her eyes. Spock observed the dematerialization without reaction.

While Radak's exit was quite interesting, Spock had noticed something very peculiar while walking around the dome's perimeter. Some of the equipment had been scavenged from a Starfleet unmanned rescue vessel—no doubt, the one that had been sent out years before, never to return.

Some of the puzzle, for him at least, was starting to fall into place.

Shallert was standing the watch in the main transporter room, duty which did not require constant vigilance, so he spent much of the time studying updated equipment manuals.

Out of the corner of his eye, he thought he saw something move on the transporter platform. He looked up. A smiling Vulcan youth stood on the reference disk. Shallert blinked, and the boy was gone. Mouth open, he checked the transporter console. It was not turned on; besides, there had been none of the characteristic sound or transporter effect.

He hesitated, then called for security on the com. "Olaus here," came the reply.

"Edward, Jonathan here. Clear out the padded cell in the brig. Are you registering an intruder?"

"No," Olaus said. "What's up? Wait a minute . . . there's a warm body in quadrant 2, deck 7 . . . nobody was there a second ago."

On deck 7 of the saucer, or primary hull, in a corridor just outside engineering and the impulse power plant, Radak walked alone, staring at this and that, marveling at the construction of the metal ship. He stretched his hand out to touch the door to engineering. It was locked, but that did not matter to Radak. It opened and he peered into the multi-level chamber. Engineering was almost empty; only one junior watch officer stood on the second level, facing the grid which divided engineering from the impulse engines. The impulse engines were shut down; very little orbital adjustment was required by the *Enterprise* at the moment, and that could be handled by the docking and positioning engines mounted at various places around the outside of the ship's engineering and primary hulls. Very quietly, very boldly, Radak strolled by the control panels without attracting the officer's notice, and quickly realized that this was not the *Enterprise*'s main power plant. He visualized the outboard nacelles housing the main propulsion units, but decided against touring them for the moment. He had been gone for thirty seconds, and it would be best to return . . .

"We're rather used to that sort of coming and going," Kirk said as soon as he had recovered. "We do it often ourselves." He was aware of the difference between transporting and what Radak had just done, but he wasn't about to reveal his astonishment to Grake.

"The boy has not been dematerialized and assembled by a transporter," T'Prylla said, stepping on to the platform. "He has had his body exactly replicated at another point in space-time, balancing the event with a complete transformation of his past structure. In essence, the individual disturbances of all his atoms have been unwound and rewound at different coordinates. Some would call it controlled coincidence. We can now master synchronicity itself, Captain."

Radak reappeared next to his mother, reached to the console, and touched another series of switches. T'Prylla stared at Spock as if searching for understanding.

"I assume," Spock said, "that the apparent identity of certain subatomic particles with like particles, wherever and whenever they may be in the universe, has been taken advantage of. What is the range of your ability to transform coordinates?"

"Under the present circumstances, two hundred kilometers," Radak said. "I was in the process of just such a transform when I encountered your first landing party."

"That would explain the anomalous tricorder readings," Chapel said.

"Would it, Spock?" Kirk asked.

"I would assume so, Captain."

"We're doing a lot of assuming here," McCoy said. "We could take advantage of this to move the sleepers to the *Enterprise . . . assuming,*" he said emphatically, "that your technique has none of the disadvantages of the transporter."

Grake shook his head. "No, Doctor. Theoretically, it is possible, but not now. At the moment, our equipment can only handle masses not much larger than my son. Not even I can be transformed, though my wife falls just within the limits. We could not transform hibernaculum and sleeper at the same time. But we are not through with our demonstration. T'Raus has been working on her own special project." He held his hand out to help his daughter onto the platform.

"At the scale of the very small—what Vulcans call *numosma* and humans call the Planck-Wheeler length—space breaks down into a maze of singularities," T'Raus said, standing at the edge of the platform with her hands clasped in front of her.

"She looks like a student about to give a piano recital," Chapel whispered to Mason. Mason thought she looked a lot more self-confident than that.

"Until now, we have had no way of studying these extremely small regions, and have had to deal with them in theory alone. Yet we know that it is at these levels that the nature of matter and energy is determined. Now, through the transformer, we can create virtual simulations of small regions of space and time—and of very large regions as well, up to the size of a universe. These simulations are correct in every detail but one—they are not themselves 'real.' Soon, we may in fact be able to recreate regions of space-time with that final touch of reality, and our work will near completion."

She was almost offhand in the way she pronounced her next words. "Our goal must be quite obvious, of course. We intend to create a new universe, on a scale where we can control and study its development. When we can do that, we will be close to understanding the most interesting period of our own universe—the first few minutes after creation. Everything after that interval has been decay and decline."

"Not quite that bad, I hope," McCoy said.

"Fascinating," Spock said.

Mason was more confused than fascinated. Kirk hardly blinked an eye.

119

T'Raus lifted an arm and touched several buttons on the console with the same easy, familiar grace of her brother. "Please watch the transparent chamber to the right of the platform. It is there that our demonstration of the very small will begin."

Chapter Sixteen

The glass sphere, mounted on a single silver rod, filled with what looked like the shadows of trees. The shadows began to whirl together, drawing dark bands around the sphere's perimeter. The bands smeared and merged until the sphere's interior was a uniform neutral gray.

"Our eyes can only perceive things they are familiar with," T'Raus said. "For that reason, most of the simulation will be lost to us. And again, because our eyes rely on light to carry information to them, what we perceive will not be totally accurate. Still, the simulation contains all the information necessary for a thorough understanding of the foundations of space-time. What we have difficulty perceiving, our machines can interpret for us." The sphere was now filled with elusive colors, rising from the neutral gray and being absorbed back into it.

Mason felt as if she were being hypnotized. Even at a distance of five or six meters, the display soon filled her field of vision. For an instant she thought she saw the sphere fill with snakes, but the snakes became clouds of floating balls. In turn, the clouds became twisting sheets of rubber—sheets soon riddled with holes which flexed inward and touched other holes. Then the sheets disappeared, leaving *only* the holes, which pulsed and seemed to both grow and shrink at once, following some outlandish rhythm both regular and chaotic. Next, the sphere was a haven for nested tunnels. The tunnels shrank and became strands of spaghetti. The spaghetti turned a wondrous blue-gray and danced so vigorously the entire dome seemed to spin around her.

Kirk saw something completely different. He was reminded of the propellers on old-fashioned airplanes—thousands and thousands spinning, varying in pitch, the blades lengthening and joining until all were connected, yet still spinning individually.

Chekov felt a kinship with what was in the sphere. He recognized it—or rather, what was controlling him recognized it, with the same bizarre nostalgia one might hold for the burned-out wreck of an old home. It made no sense to Chekov, but he participated nevertheless.

Chapel saw an infinity of bizarre flowers, their petals linking and unlinking.

Spock made an effort to see only what was there. He could not. There was nothing real in the sphere, nothing on to which he could hook the rigid logic of his race. He was instantly and uncomfortably aware of the limits of his conditioning; Vulcans sought total logic in a universe built on controlled chaos. The effort ultimately had to be futile. The display saddened him, depressed him, aroused his human half . . .

And he suddenly became aware of the paradox. Vulcans had done this research, ostensibly; created these displays. T'Prylla, for all her unorthodox methods of logic, was still as constrained as he was, perhaps moreso. Such researches should have been extremely difficult, perhaps impossible for her, for any Vulcan.

Then who, or what, had performed the research? The human physicists who might have aided the researchers and shared such insights were all in cold storage. Spock turned away from the sphere, unwilling to tolerate much more.

McCoy turned away also, for similar reasons. For him the sphere was filled with faces, and the faces were turning into skulls, the eye-sockets of the skulls elongating into infinite corridors of death and misery, the teeth glinting and flashing. The insight that forced him to turn away was that all the stars in the universe were simply reflections from the teeth of skulls. The sphere showed him how he could go mad, if he ever lost control.

T'Raus touched the buttons lightly, and the sphere once again became a vacant ball of glass. Throughout the demonstration the observers had been completely silent, and the silence lingered.

Kirk spoke first. "I'm not sure I'm capable of judging your accomplishment," he said, touching his hand to his forehead. "Breakthrough or not, I also fail to see what all this has to do with our immediate problem."

Radak stood near Kirk. He turned slowly toward the captain, his face betraying very un-Vulcan signs of agitation. "In a year, our mastery will be so complete that we can duplicate the bodies of our sleepers without the apparatus on your ship, without any machinery at all. All this will be discarded, and with our minds alone we can travel wherever we wish, transform anything." He stared fixedly at Kirk. "We will no longer be confined to our planetoid, nor will we require Federation starships."

That is not the truth! T'Prylla agonized, struggling to break through to Spock, anybody. Corona would finish its work long before such things could be accomplished.

Kirk turned to Grake. "Does your son speak for all of you?" Grake and T'Prylla nodded simultaneously. "I can appreciate the magnitude of your . . . future accomplishment," Kirk continued. "But I have to deal with present realities. And Federation law dictates that I do everything in my power to save its citizens from harm. The sleepers are in danger. We must do as our medical expert says. I . . . I can guarantee that your fears for their safety are unwarranted. They will not be injured during their journey to the *Enterprise*." McCoy nodded with satisfaction.

"There are several more things which must be done to our shuttle to make travel completely safe for the sleepers," Spock said. "We will return to the *Enterprise*, perform the final installations, and ferry the sleepers as soon as possible."

"Very well," T'Prylla said, acquiescing with a nod.

That, Mason thought, was entirely too quick and easy after all the objections they had made . . .

Chekov returned to the storage dome first. Wah Ching and Pauli stood outside the boarding tube. He conferred with them briefly, then walked down the tube and closed the shuttle hatch.

Inside the small craft, he looked around with drugged slowness and walked forward through the passenger cabin to the pilot's seat and control panel. With a service hex wrench, he unfastened the top cover and peered at the maze of glass cables and power beam guides. He took his phaser and set the beam for minimum width, shallow penetration. At low power, the phaser would spall insulation off the beam guides. The shuttle self-diagnosing system would detect a fault, but since there were no sensors directly attached to the insulation, the shuttle computer would not be able to explain the trouble, only to locate it. It would be difficult to notice any difference just by looking . . .

The shuttle would be disabled.

He fought every step of the way, until his body ran rivers of sweat . . . but to no avail.

He belted the phaser, mopped his forehead with his sleeve, and opened the hatch. He put on an angry face and stormed back through the tube. "Who's been in here?" The guards looked at him, astonished. "The panel cover is open," he said. Kirk, Spock, McCoy, Chapel and Mason walked across the decking. Chekov approached them, wishing he could simply die and get the misery over with. "Mr. Spock . . ." he began.

Spock emerged from the shuttle and shook his head. "I suspect sabotage, Captain."

McCoy swore under his breath. "I feel like we're wading through glue, Jim. They're thwarting everything we do."

Kirk glanced across the storage dome. "Spock, run a tricorder check for listening devices or . . . anything else suspicious. Chekov, keep a guard on the dome entrance."

Spock ran his check and announced there were no detectable listening devices. "But I cannot guarantee we will speak in privacy."

"Then we'll take the risk. Spock, what in hell is going on here?"

"Something is seriously wrong, Jim. I have seen equipment in the research dome which I am certain was removed from the unmanned rescue probe. Apparently, at the time of the probe's arrival, Station One was reluctant to be rescued, but in need of all available instrumentation and raw material. Furthermore, the station personnel are not behaving as Vulcans should behave. They are not even behaving like insane Vulcans. The excuses they offer are weak and contradictory. The children appear to be more in control than Grake and T'Prylla, and that is totally uncharacteristic."

"Couldn't that be explained by the isolation?" Mason asked.

"No," Spock said. "There is a pattern to their behavior, but it does not match any pattern for my people. It is the pattern of a controlling presence, with goals dissimilar to our own."

"But there's no life here," McCoy said. "We know protostar clouds are completely sterile. Oh, there are the usual organic molecules—"

"I do not believe they are being controlled by an organic life form," Spock said. "The evidence points to something very knowledgable, very interested in the processes the researchers claim to have mastered."

"Any ideas what that might be?"

"I suggest we contact the *Enterprise* and see how Mr. Scott is doing with the transporter. I doubt that he has found anything wrong. If my hypothesis is correct, the transporter is in perfect working order, but the beam itself is being tampered with. That could explain my clumsy arrival in the station, and it could also explain Ensign Chekov's difficulties."

"Then what the hell are we going to do?" McCoy asked.

"We are going to play our hidden ace, Dr. McCoy. We are going to request materials be sent down to repair the shuttle."

Veblen looked at the algorithm models, biting his lower lip. Half on impulse, he typed on the keyboard. *Are you serious?*

These are the best models the stochastic algorithm can currently produce, the computer replied on the screen. Veblen had shut the voice off; he much preferred working with displays. It was so much easier to track programming errors.

"Mr. Veblen to the bridge," Uhura called over the com. Veblen transferred the model data to his portable notepad and ran for the turbolift.

Scott was on the bridge, talking to Kirk in the station. "I find Mr. Spock's conclusions a great relief," he said.

"We don't," Kirk said laconically. "Is Veblen there?"

"Present, Captain," Veblen said.

"Mr. Veblen, Spock has a special request for shuttle repair parts." Veblen and Scott looked at each other; Veblen was certainly not the man to handle parts replacement.

"Mr. Veblen," Spock said, "the *Galileo II* requires the following kits." Spock recited twenty-six separate kit numbers, apparently from memory. Veblen took them down quickly, then handed them to Scott. Scott looked them over. Only five had anything to do with the shuttle, and none, surprisingly, with the hibernacula. "I am also interested in how the algorithms are adjusting to the new data. Has there been an advancement of model C in probability?"

Veblen's eyes widened. "There has indeed, Mr. Spock. Model C is now the prime model, with enhancements. The Ybakra—"

"Thank you, Mr. Veblen. Please expedite the delivery of the parts. Until the shuttle is repaired, we are confined to the station." Spock signed off and Scott shook his head.

"What are they requesting, Mr. Scott?" Veblen asked.

"Some of the kits will replace beam guide insulators in the shuttle instrument panels. That makes sense. But these other kits—they go together to create an Ybakra isolation field."

"For the sleepers?"

"I don't think so," Scott said. "Or Dr. McCoy would have mentioned field dimensions. I don't believe these will create a large enough field for two hibernacula."

Veblen hefted his notepad thoughtfully. "Model C, I believe, has been confirmed."

T'Prylla experienced the irritation at one remove, but Corona's indecision was more immediately distressing. She was jerked back and forth, sent first to do this, then that. She had never felt Corona so confused and uncertain. She worked for a time adding more machinery to the equipment in the research dome. Briefly, she saw Grake doing similar work. T'Kosa and Anauk, she sensed, were waiting outside the storage dome. T'Raus and Radak were nowhere to be seen.

The Vulcan children stood beneath the purple nebula sky, watching a horizon-to-horizon ribbon of green unwrap at zenith. It was nothing significant, simply the unveiling of a deeper region of gas, but it served for a moment to distract Corona. Of all the things in this strange, ancient realm, the clouds of dust and gas in the nebula were most pleasing. Their abstraction reminded it of . . .

But there was no conclusion to the thought. T'Raus touched the rock again and opened the Eye-to-Stars. Its goal was so close, but time was growing short. Where would the next appearance be?

The Eye-to-Stars was more than a telescope. It searched across probable universes, as well as the distances of space and time. The only probable universe it could not scan was on the line of present reality; Corona could not know the exact outcome of its work.

In the early years, Corona had sought out young, amorphous galaxies buried in hot clouds of gas—but had not found any. Instead, it had found evidence of its own handiwork, its own halting experiments and mistakes—buried in the ancient past, barely visible across the light-eons. After nine years of patient search, feeling a growing frustration and awareness of its limits, it had found the region where it would be most likely to make its next appearance, if it should fail in the Black Box Nebula.

In the beginning, it had had an easier time of things. Conditions had been hostile, but not nearly as hostile as they were now. Now, Corona had to rely on yet another unlikely conjunction of sub-spacial masses and collapsing protostars. Just such a region had been found by the Eye-to-Stars.

But it knew the opportunities there were unlikely to be as satisfying as those in the Black Box. In fact, nothing in all its strange travels could compare. The novelty of the situation lay not in the nebula itself—a rather typical starwomb—but in the Vulcan visitors, in living and intelligent beings made of *matter*. Corona had never encountered such before. It had no idea how widespread organic intelligence would be in the future, on the next leg of its journey. So getting the work done now was extremely important.

And all it needed was a few more hours, unhindered, a miniscule length of the bizarre dimension that time had become in this old corpse of a universe.

But how would it continue its work in the dome, and deal with the new, troublesome visitors?

It was this indecision which affected T'Prylla worst of all. Finally, Corona made a choice. The visitors were much too dangerous. They could destroy some of the most useful information it had gathered if they removed the sleepers. If they managed to repair the shuttle, the transfer would begin . . .

Corona had learned too late that humans resisted its intrusions even more than adult Vulcans. Only by slightly rearranging his qualities in the transporter beam had it been able to gain control of the one called Chekov, and that by a stroke of luck. The new half-Vulcan combined the worst properties of Vulcans and humans; the first few times in the beam had been insufficient to control Spock.

But Corona had learned from failures. If Spock used the transporter just one more time . .

Scott had trouble controlling tne direction of the beam. It veered wildly first one direction, then another. Veblen watched the chief engineer swearing and adjusting the control slides. There was nothing in the beam but a test device; the kits Spock had requested were stacked on two floating pallets near the transporter platform. "Is there any transporter effect?" Veblen asked Kirk.

"None yet," the captain replied. "Wait a minute . . . just a trace."

"Aligning the beam," Scott said grimly. "It whips about like a snake. The probe should be assembling . . . now."

"Here it comes," Kirk said. "It's intact!"

"Bringing it back," Scott said. When the probe had returned, he motioned for Shallert to position the pallets over the reference and number two disks.

"We're preparing to send the kits now," Veblen said. He checked the display on his portable terminal, hooked up to the ship's computers. The erratic beam behavior was being analyzed in detail to provide more data to confirm and expand on Model C.

"Whatever's mucking with the beam must be operating a field as wide as the planetoid itself," Scott said.

Veblen's display indicated the field was much wider than that, perhaps as much as a hundred thousand kilometers in diameter. The picture he was constructing of it showed a complex structure on several levels, operating in both status geometry, subspace and at least three fraction-space geodesics. The *Enterprise*'s sensors were now alert to certain clues, sweeping deep into the Black Box, toward the murky triplet of infant stars.

"Sending now," Scott said. "And I'm glad it's not people I'm sending."

"Effect beginning," Kirk said. "We're getting two assembly patterns . . . they're forming. Down and intact!"

Scott cut the transporter beam and stretched his arms out to relieve muscle tension. He groaned and smiled at Veblen. "Like taking a boat through a storm," he said.

"A very interesting storm, too," Veblen said. "I'd certainly like to talk with Mr. Spock about it, but nobody seems willing to engage in a straight conversation down there."

The sensors had traced the origin of the field. Wrapped in an intense oblate spheroid of Ybakra radiation, the three young stars—orbiting each other across distances of hundreds of millions of miles—were themselves the source.

Chapter Seventeen

Kirk and Spock assembled the Ybakra cage within the shuttle's cargo compartment, without comment or any clue as to what they were planning. Indeed, to a great extent Kirk himself didn't know. When they were through, Chekov and McCoy inspected the device—Chekov paying particular attention. The shield was a cubic cage about two meters on a side, made of black pipe with smaller red cubes at each of the eight corners.

Mason sat on a fold-down chair opposite the cargo doors, watching the proceedings disconsolately. She had never felt so useless and out-of-place. They were obviously in trouble, but she wasn't a part of the team; they couldn't confide in her, or give her something to do. She was excess baggage. Chapel gave her a reassuring smile, but for all her sincerity it only deepened her distress.

"Now for a test," Kirk said. "We'll need somebody inside holding a tricorder. Bones?"

"Not me," McCoy said. "I outrank Chekov. Let him stand inside."

Chekov's face paled noticeably. Spock held the tricorder out to him, but he backed off a step, hands raised.

"There's no danger," Kirk said, eyes narrowing. "It's just to protect the hibernacula."

There was no way out of it without raising a scene. For the first time, Chekov knew that the alien will within him was unable to control things completely. It contemplated creating a commotion in the dome, but decided the risks were too small to get upset about. It forced Chekov to smile.

He accepted the tricorder and stepped into the cage. "Switch on," Kirk said. Spock flipped a switch on the top of an upper cube. There was no sound or any other effect; the cube was simply cut off from exposure to Ybakra.

Chekov collapsed. McCoy instinctively made a move to enter the cube but Kirk restrained him. "Jim, he's—"

"Wait a moment, just a moment," Kirk said. "Spock?"

"I believe my hypothesis is correct, Jim. Ybakra radiation carries the controlling messages. Chekov has not been himself the past few hours." Spock stepped through the shield and knelt next to Chekov. The ensign's eyelids fluttered and opened and he stared at Spock with an expression of blissful relief. "Mr. Spock . . . bad, so very awful and horrible . . ."

Spock motioned for McCoy to join them. McCoy ran his tricorder over Chekov and pronounced him fit, but exhausted from severe nervous strain. "I've been fighting," Chekov said softly.

"Fighting what?" Kirk asked.

"Taking me over. Making me . . . I sabotaged, it sabotaged the shuttle . . ."

"We know," Kirk said. "Spock had switched the security recorders on. You were caught in the act. What does . . . it . . . feel like? What is it?"

"I don't know," Chekov said. "Deliberate, very

133

large . . . angry, searching. I don't know." His eyes closed.

"He should be in the sickbay," McCoy said.

"He cannot be moved from the shield, or he will be controlled again," Spock said.

"When did it take him over?" Kirk asked.

"I believe I felt its presence just before I collapsed after transporting," Spock said. "I assume it was able to take command of Mr. Chekov in the transporter beam. That would explain the delay before his assembly on the *Enterprise.*"

"Why didn't it take over all of us, then?" Kirk asked. His quick glance at Mason made her straighten in her seat. She was about to protest, but Spock cut her off.

"Perhaps it was adjusting to humans. So far, it has only controlled Vulcans. Much as I dislike the idea, it may have an easier time assuming control of Vulcans than humans . . . though why I was spared, I don't know."

"Your human blood, no doubt," McCoy said. "Does this mean everyone in the station is possessed?" He injected a nutritive restorer solution into Chekov's arm and stood up.

"That's what we have to assume," Kirk said. "By whom, or what . . . or to what end, is anybody's guess."

"We do know some things about the influence," Spock said. "It uses Ybakra radiation, which we have always thought to have a negligible effect on human nervous systems, and a relatively minor effect on Vulcans—unless, of course, high exposure occurs under cold storage conditions. Apparently the effect can be more profound. I have already notified Mr. Veblen that Model C has increased in probability—"

"What in the devil is 'Model C'?" McCoy asked.

"Mr. Veblen's stochastic algorithms produced some rather far-fetched models, which we originally rejected. Model C postulated that the inhabitants of the station had been taken over by some outside agency. The algorithm returned to the model when we fed it more information about Ybakra radiation and the behavior of station personnel. The model, I believe, is now confirmed."

"At least the ship is aware something's going on," Kirk said. "Do we dare tell them everything?"

Spock nodded. "It may already be too late to disguise our awareness. What we must do is take advantage of any confusion the being might be feeling, with the loss of its sole human puppet. We must bring one of the Vulcans here, by force if necessary. I would suggest T'Prylla."

"Any suggestions as to how?" McCoy asked.

"By gentle persuasion, if at all possible. If it still has doubts, we must play on them."

"How can I help?" Mason asked. Kirk turned and shook his head.

"By maintaining your objectivity," he said sharply. "You're an observer. Observe."

"Jim . . ." McCoy said, but Kirk waved his hand.

"We're in very deep trouble, Bones," he said. "I'll tender any apologies later."

In orbit around the planetoid, the *Enterprise* once again passed over the station within the two hundred kilometer limit. Radak appeared briefly in several of the ship's cabins and corridors, found them occupied, and finally materialized in a narrow, deserted service corridor below the ship's computer, between decks 8 and 9. Light cables and beam guides clustered thickly on the walls and ceiling. There was no artificial gravitation in the service corridor, so the boy floated for a moment while deciding what to do next.

Suddenly, as if a finger had been lopped off, Corona lost one of its extensions. The human called Chekov was no longer under its control.

Corona had focused too much of its attention on Radak. Things were happening on the station. Yet it could not just withdraw Radak from the *Enterprise*, not when there was such an opportunity to learn. If there was a way to control the ship itself, its problems would be over. It would be allowed to finish its work. But now the humans were approaching T'Prylla, and it could sense the Vulcan female was about to make her move.

Radak had been under the control of Corona for so long that it was possible to release the young Vulcan for hours at a stretch, to carry out commands already given. In a sense, Radak, T'Raus and Corona had developed together, and their relationship was fixed; without the young Vulcans, Corona would not have had a sense of place and time, not in the way these organic beings had. They acted as conduits through which it could perceive and interpret what the other Vulcans and humans did. Radak would be left aboard the ship to finish his task; Corona shifted its full attention to the station, but not in time to prevent further disaster.

"There is no need for me to inspect your work," T'Prylla said in the *reshek* corridor. Kirk and Spock stood on each side of her. McCoy and Mason stood behind them.

"We wish to demonstrate how safe the sleepers will be in the shuttle," Spock said.

"That is more for T'Kosa to determine," T'Prylla said. She looked at Spock, and for the briefest moment, Spock saw a glimmer of rebellious awareness, a personality behind the mask. T'Prylla's lips moved, saying "Force me," silently in Vulcan. The mask returned almost immediately.

"Nurse Chapel, take her left arm," Spock said. Chapel grabbed the arm and held it tightly. "Doctor, the right."

McCoy held the right and Spock reached for her shoulder. T'Prylla's body gave a sudden jerk and she slammed McCoy and Chapel against a bulkhead.

Chapel fell back, stunned, and Kirk moved in to take her place. Mason jumped to one side as the recorder deftly maneuvered out of everybody's way. Spock grabbed T'Prylla's shoulder and pinched it sharply. Her upper body contorted but she did not collapse. McCoy brought out his subcutane and tried to place it against her arm. She whipped around violently, her breath ragged, her face darkening to brown. McCoy found his opening and the subcutane connected, injecting its tranquilizer. Kirk and McCoy released her and stepped back. She leaned against the bulkhead, chest heaving. She tried to stand straight but couldn't. It was awful to see her struggling, especially for Mason, who was reminded of an injured animal resisting the ministrations of its keepers. Then T'Prylla seemed to wilt. Nine years of almost constant possession could not prevent the action of McCoy's drug. Spock and McCoy caught her as she slumped.

"So much for subtle persuasion," McCoy said.

"We must get her to the shuttle immediately," Spock said. Kirk drew his phaser and set it for stun. With his other hand, he opened his communicator.

"Kirk to *Enterprise*."

"*Enterprise*. Uhura here, Captain."

"Move the ship out to a synchronous orbit. Now."

"Yes, sir."

"And tell Scott—"

The communicator crackled. He adjusted it, but to no avail. "Interference," he said. On a hunch, he turned the phaser on a bulkhead and tried to fire it. The button produced no effect whatsoever.

"It is indeed a master of energy," Spock said. Kirk belted the useless weapon. He reached out to help Spock and McCoy lift T'Prylla; Mason lent her shoulder to Chapel.

Olaus had passed word to Scott; they still had a track on the intruder. Veblen came on the bridge with Shallert and they watched the forward screen as the ship's internal scanners displayed the unsecured sector.

"He's in the service corridor under the ship's computer," Scott said tersely. "Recognize him?"

"He's the one I saw in the transporter room," Shallert said. "Thought I was going crazy . . . until now. How did he get there?"

"I don't know," Scott said. "Mr. Olaus and I aren't quite sure what we should do with him."

"Tell security to stay away from him," Veblen said.

Scott looked at the staff officer with a dubious expression. "He's in the middle of the ship's most delicate equipment."

"They should at least stay out of sight. We're tracking him; we can stop him before he does anything disastrous, if that's what he's here for. We need to know more about him—or whatever's controlling him. What they want to do."

"I canna' accept that risk," Scott said. "Scott to security team A. Move into the corridor and attempt capture."

The service corridor formed a circle around and beneath the computer. Devereaux and his men had pressed themselves against the equipment insulation plates around the curve from where Radak floated. Now they gripped the guide ropes and pulled themselves swiftly and silently along.

Radak was aware there was trouble on the station, but he had been temporarily left to himself. He knew what he was looking for, and what he had to do when he found it—Corona could rely on Radak. He peered behind the beam guides for the ship's central data conduit, not yet aware of the security men approaching from behind.

When Kirk's abrupt transmission was received, Scott acted on the orders immediately. The *Enterprise* accelerated and pushed herself into a higher orbit, maneuvering until she was in synchronous movement with the station four thousand kilometers below. The whole action took less than five minutes, and in that time—

Radak twisted around, stared at the guards, and tried to transform back to the station. He could not transform by himself, however, and Corona had not yet returned. The guards floated toward him, phasers drawn. He tried to deactivate the phasers, but he could not. He backed away, feeling his weakness acutely. Then he realized the ship was moving, that he was already too far from the station to be transformed even if Corona did return.

"He's not doing anything," Scott said.

"Maybe we have him," Veblen said.

Devereaux backed the boy up against the end of the corridor. "We're not going to hurt you," he said. "How in hell did you get here in the first place?"

For the first time in ten years, Radak felt completely lost. His instructions said nothing about how to behave if he was captured.

Chapter Eighteen

They lay T'Prylla in the cage next to Chekov. McCoy changed the ampule in the subcutane and injected her with an antidote to the tranquilizer. "She'll come around in a few minutes," he said. "But she'll be weak for an hour or so."

"I wonder if any Vulcan can ever be weak," Chapel said, massaging her shoulder.

"Ceptain, I do not think she is the center of the being," Chekov said. "I think it concentrates on the children."

T'Prylla's eyes opened. She stared intently at Spock. "Nine years, three months, two days and twelve hours," she said. "That is how long we have been slaves. My gratitude, Spock." She tried to sit up but her arms collapsed under her. Mason held her shoulders as she fell back.

"I have many questions," Spock said, "and not much time to obtain answers."

"Then the questions must wait. For all that time, I have been considering ways to overcome Corona."

"Corona?" Kirk asked.

"Yes. It manifests as a huge corona of Ybakra radiation emanating from the infant stars. It has a specific purpose—to create a new universe—and we must not allow it to succeed. Spock, Radak was the first to be taken over. T'Raus was next. Through the children, it extended its control to the rest of us. You must touch minds with Radak. You must communicate directly with Corona—force it to listen—or it will never understand."

"How do you force an all-powerful, hostile intelligence to listen?" McCoy asked.

"It is neither all-powerful, nor hostile," T'Prylla said. "It is merely dedicated. It is the last of its kind, and there will be no more like it unless it succeeds. It is quite weak—it is not accustomed to a realm of matter, and only through us can it manipulate small amounts of matter."

"Yet it is a master of energy, of space and time," Spock said.

"You have deduced that much. We could never have come so far in our researches without its help—yet I can hardly say the new machines belong to us, or fulfill our work. Spock! You must find Radak, and you must administer *ka nifoor*."

"What's that?" Kirk asked.

"He was just a child when he was taken over," Spock said. "Neither he nor T'Raus have undergone the discipline of Vulcan adulthood. If I can administer *ka nifoor*, it is possible the being's influence will wane."

"It controls all of us through them," T'Prylla said.

Spock looked troubled.

"Well, Spock?" Kirk asked.

"There is also the possibility the being will occupy my mind," Spock said. "I have resisted so far, though I am not certain why—"

"You just won't admit it," McCoy said.

"Doctor, Chekov is totally human, and it possessed him quite effectively."

"In the beam of the transporter," T'Prylla said.

141

"Which is why we aren't going to use the trans-porter," Kirk said. Outside the shuttle, there was a high-pitched whining sound, followed by a sharp, loud *crack*. "What in hell was that?"

Wah Ching ran down the boarding tube, phaser drawn. "Captain, they're all in the storage dome—all but the boy. They're heading this way!"

"Get Pauli inside the shuttle," Kirk said. "Spock, we're going back."

"Yes, sir." Spock went forward to the shuttle controls. T'Prylla was now strong enough to sit up on her own, and Mason released her, instinctively wiping her hands on her pants.

Pauli rolled into the ship just as the boarding tube seal separated. The shuttle was filled with roaring as air exploded through the crack. Mason screamed in silence, holding her ears with both hands and keeping her eyes tightly shut. Pauli rebounded from a bulkhead and reached up to slap the hatch lever down. Air screamed into the cabin from emergency repressurization valves, and Mason felt the horrible, straining emptiness in her lungs fill until she could breathe normally.

"They tried to kill us!" Pauli shouted hoarsely. The shuttle's landing lifters pushed them a few meters off the station platform.

McCoy quickly looped cargo cables across the deck and over Chekov and T'Prylla. "Get into a seat!" he shouted at Mason and Chapel. "And secure that damned machine!" Mason pulled the recorder forward and slammed it against a magnetic grip. She buckled herself in just in time to avoid a lurch which propelled McCoy across the cargo compartment. The Ybakra cage creaked ominously.

Kirk grabbed hold of the navigator's chair and steadied himself. "They're not going to let us go without a fight."

Spock struggled with the controls. Warning buzzers sounded and alert lights came on across the instrument panel.

"Didn't we fix it?" McCoy called from the passenger cabin as he fell into a seat.

Kirk's communicator beeped. He strapped himself in and flipped the device open. "Kirk here."

"Captain! We've been trying to get through for hours—"

"Scotty! Lock a tractor on to the shuttle! Pull us in!"

"We canna', not at this angle through the planetoid, Captain. What's happening?"

Kirk glanced at Spock for an explanation. "Our engines are being neutralized," Spock said grimly. "We will not be able to lift off. It does not wish to let T'Prylla go."

"Scotty," Kirk said. "This may be a mistake, but can you get a transporter fix on us?"

"Aye, that I can. But—"

"Risk it, Scotty! Get everyone in the shuttle aboard the *Enterprise*—and the Ybakra shield, as well!" Kirk met Spock's questioning glance and shrugged. "Either way, Spock . . . let's just hope Corona doesn't have its mind on the transporter."

As the transporter effect started, Mason began to pray, gripping the chair arms tightly. She closed her eyes. Across the aisle, McCoy let out a long and expressive string of expletives . . .

The shuttle fell from an altitude of two hundred meters and crashed onto the scarred gray surface of the planetoid.

"We have them all," Shallert announced from the transporter room. "But the goddamned thing's interfering again!"

"Isolate each form-memory," Scott said grimly from the elevator. Veblen rode beside him.

"They're isolated. We're racking up delay time . . . thirty seconds."

"Triage," Veblen said.

"How's that, Mr. Veblen?" Scott demanded. The elevator doors opened and the engineer leaped to

143

the transporter controls. Shallert transferred the controls and Scott began to play them like the keys of a piano. Veblen stayed to one side, watching the fitful sparklings above the assigned disks.

"I've already dumped the radiation cage," Shallert explained. "Even so . . ."

"We only have a firm grip on seven," Scott said, looking as if he were about to cry. "It's wrestling us for them!" The transporter whined and groaned alternately. The air became thick with the sweet electric smell of unrealized transporter ghosts, and a special ventilator switched on. "Ye canna' ha' them, damn ye!" Scott screamed, pulling all the slides down at once and switching for emergency power. The transporter room floor hummed and one of the unassigned disks began to smoke.

One by one, the assigned disks displayed transporter effects, until seven were occupied. The remaining two showed clear shafts of white light, signifying lost signals. Even before the effects were well formed, Scott redirected the two stray people. "I'm sending 'em to the station," he said. "They canna' return to the shuttle. I'm sending 'em back and God help them get there in one piece."

Corona gave up its attempt to control all the form-memories in the transporter beam. The task was simply too much without the help of Radak and T'Prylla; Corona felt their loss keenly. Even though it realized T'Prylla was one of those in the beam, her data was confused with the form-memory of the cage, and Corona could not differentiate them in so little time.

By the time the cage was cut from the beam, Corona had already concentrated on two others in the beam, separating them. The half-Vulcan, half-human science officer, Spock, and the only other female in the group, Mason, began to assemble in the storage dome, where Scott had redirected them.

Corona reached deep into the form-memory of Spock, and exulted . . .

Kirk, McCoy, Chapel, T'Prylla, Chekov and the two guards lay fully formed on the transporter platform. Kirk got up on his knees and looked at the other disks. "Spock? The girl? Where are they?"

Scott's expression was pitiful. "I couldna' hold them, Captain. There was too much interference."

Kirk cringed and held his head in his hands. He looked up almost immediately and asked where the cage was.

"Dropped from the beam," Shallert said.

"We'll need another. A large one—and some portable shields, too." He stood above Chekov and T'Prylla on adjacent disks, looking down on them suspiciously. McCoy helped T'Prylla to her feet while Kirk and Shallert saw to Chekov and the two guards.

"Get stretchers up here," McCoy said, looking around for someone to take his orders and fixing on Veblen. "And get sickbay ready!" Veblen nodded and went to the wall com to relay the commands.

Kirk opened and closed his hands helplessly, then bounded on still-shaky legs for the elevator. Veblen followed, reaching out to steady him as he wobbled. The doors closed. "Bridge," Kirk said.

"Captain, we've captured the Vulcan boy, Radak. Somehow he reached the *Enterprise* and was found in the service corridor below the computer center. And as for Ybakra shields—the boy is in one right now. We've shielded an entire brig cell."

"Then we have two of Corona's main extensions," Kirk said. "And Radak was the one T'Prylla wanted Spock to touch minds with . . ." He shook his head fiercely. "We may be in worse trouble than we think, Mr. Veblen. T'Prylla said something down there that scares me, especially after what we saw."

"Captain, I'll need as much information as possible to feed the algorithms."

Kirk looked at Veblen from the corner of his eye, prepared to tell the computer officer to go to hell, and take his algorithms with him. But he controlled his anger and worry and nodded. "On the bridge," he said. "I'll put as much as I can into the log while we're deciding what to do next."

Spock rolled onto his back, his eyes tightly shut. Mason had assembled on her feet, and she looked around with no real comprehension of what had happened. Where was the transporter room, where was the *Enterprise?* She was in the storage dome— and the dome was empty. Then she saw Spock struggling near her feet, moaning.

Oh my God, she thought. Now was the time to panic. She was alone in the station, alone with Vulcans . . .

Spock controlled his writhing and opened his eyes. He rose to his knees and shook his head, then braced a hand on the floor and pushed himself upright. He looked dazed, preoccupied. His lips worked and he closed his eyes again. "I need help," he said.

Mason backed away, hands clutching her throat.

"I am about to be controlled by Corona," he said. "I only have a few minutes of resistance left. You must . . . help . . ."

He swiveled and held out a tense, half-closed hand.

"Please," Mason said.

"I can feel it in my mind. I can hear its thoughts. It does not know how to listen . . . It does not respect us. We are here only for its use. And it is about to destroy . . . everything." His eyes widened.

He's afraid, Mason realized. *He's seen something and it terrifies him!* Whatever reserves of pragmatism and toughness remained in her, evaporated. She was a little girl again, listening to scary stories about incredible off-world monstrosities, alien horrors, unseen inhuman demons. Standing before her was living proof of all the stories—an alien, strange and repugnant, himself taken over by a demon. The storytellers on Yalbo had told the truth!

"I cannot hold it back. I must enter a trance state. But I cannot do that . . ." Spock's expression was pleading. "You must take part of me within you." He twisted in agony, arms held up in the air, and shouted a string of Vulcan words. She backed away two more steps, horrified—and fascinated. "I must pass on the ritual. It is not aware . . . it is blind inside me while I resist . . . I can pass everything on to you, give you instructions, a temporary part of my mind—"

"NO!" But she did not back away any farther.

Spock shuddered and appeared to draw himself together. "I am aware of your prejudices. I am aware of your fear. You must overcome them. Your life, your existence . . . perhaps the existence of our entire universe . . . are at stake. We are not enemies. I need your courage!" He reached both hands out to her.

All right, a voice said away from all her repulsion and horror. *Time to cut the crap and get down to business, don't you think? You can either live the rest of your life—however short that may be—slipping and sliding on all the muck your fellow Yalbans laid down for you, or you can rise above it. You can help the nasty, alien Vulcan, whom you've come to know and respect, underneath all your stupid bigotry, or you can let everything go to hell. Your one chance, Small-Planet Girl.*

She took a step forward, her stomach contracting to a tiny ball. Everything was elongated and strange. She grasped Spock's warm, dry hands and guided them to her temples. He lowered one hand and clasped the base of her neck. He said something in Vulcan and there was a fire in her brain, writing very tiny letters over every available centimeter of darkness . . .

And then she understood his Vulcan words:

"You have the courage and grace of an *ahkor,*" he

had said, and through Spock she remembered the most beautiful, the largest, the brightest bird she had ever seen, its feathers copper and gold and chrome, its eye red as the sun, flying over the sand and jagged, smoking mountains of Vulcan.

Part of the Vulcan was inside her.

He lay on the floor, limp, his face peaceful. He was locked in trance, useless to Corona.

But, along with Spock, she could feel another touch, weak but still present.

Corona—or some part of it—had also made the transition. She was now not one, but three . . .

Chapter Nineteen

The guard cleared the brig field from his path and Kirk entered the cell. T'Prylla sat with Radak in one corner, on furniture transferred from the rec room; Chekov sat in the opposite corner, still de-briefing onto a ship's log notepad. A makeshift curtain had been arranged across the diagonal for some privacy; it wasn't much for luxury, however, and Kirk felt called upon to apologize.

"We understand perfectly," T'Prylla said. She touched her son's shoulder. "You have returned Radak to me. That is luxury enough for the time being. What has happened at the station?"

"Spock and Mason didn't make it back with us. We assume they are in the storage dome, but we simply don't know. Uh . . . Corona is blocking all transmissions and jamming all sensor readings." His face was pale and lined with worry; he hadn't even changed uniforms after the narrow escape.

"We are all in very great danger," T'Prylla said calmly. She looked at Radak. "I know the broad outlines of Corona's plans, but my son is much

149

better informed. He will not tell us, however." Radak regarded Kirk with icy contempt. "Corona apparently gave him some measure of autonomy, and he is waiting for his contact to resume. It is all he has known for ten years."

"I'm worried about two things," Kirk said. "Most immediately, the fate of Mason and Spock. And this attempt of Corona's to create another universe. I don't like the sound of that."

"Nor do I, Captain," T'Prylla said. "I assume that it means Corona would like to re-create conditions he is more familiar with."

"And what might those be?"

"Corona is a fugitive, Captain. And a kind of scientist. His world ended fifteen billion years ago . . . when it gave birth to our own."

It was all well and good to be brave in the abstract. She had always been impulsive. But there were parts of her mind not nearly as noble and flexible as her conscious self, and right now they were twisting her thoughts into knots. Spock's distinctive voice spoke within her, trying to reassure.

—Do not be afraid. I have abstracted knowledge from Corona—stolen it, if you will. That is what you feel.

—(confusion, panic) *You are in my* mind!

—You are in control. I am only knowledge, not Spock. I can only suggest, and answer questions. I am like the monitors aboard the *Enterprise,* except that I cannot even veto your actions. Spock is in a trance. I am only part, a very small part, of him, within you.

Mason stood unsteadily, feeling worse than if she had discovered maggots erupting from her skin. How much of her memory was available to him—details of her life, her intimate moments, her embarrassments and shames?

—What do you know about me?

150

—Nothing. It is not important that I know. But we must do several things . . .

—I . . . don't . . . think . . . I . . . can . . . *take* . . . *this* . . .

—There is very little time. Grake, T'Raus and the others will return soon, and we must be prepared. You are temporarily safe from Corona's intrusion. It cannot take you over now, and it will not try. Here is what we must do first—

—*Vulcan!* Get out of my *mind!*

Suddenly, there was nothing. Just herself, and silence. She couldn't even feel the wisp of complete unfamiliarity that had been Corona's trace within her. Across the dome, she heard footsteps. T'Raus and T'Kosa materialized on each side of her. Grake and Anauk entered the dome through the hatchway.

Mason glanced between the two females, her jaw muscles clenched to still a scream. Moaning sounds came from her throat. Her fingers dug into the fabric of her pants and the flesh beneath.

Grake and Anauk picked up Spock's limp form and carried him toward the hatchway. T'Raus touched Mason's elbow.

"Come with us," she said.

Mason didn't move.

"We mean you no harm."

It was an effort to push one foot forward. Something was rising behind the fear, however—something even more irrational and stubborn. What would *Vulcans* think if she acted like a coward? What would the Spock within her think? T'Kosa took her by the arm and she shrugged the hand away. "Leave me alone!" she growled.

"You cannot stay here," T'Kosa said calmly. "The boarding tube emergency seal is defective. Air is leaking out. We must close off this dome." Mason turned and saw the hatch to the landing pad tube. A small crack in one corner was rimed with white; the hissing was quite loud.

Then Spock's voice returned—gentle, unobtrusive.

—You must touch T'Raus. She must be given the discipline of *ka nifoor*.

"All right! All right!" Mason said. —All right . . .

T'Prylla took Radak by the shoulders and lifted him to his feet. She was neither rough nor gentle; she simply handled her defiant son in the most efficient manner possible. Radak did not resist. She spoke to him in Vulcan. The boy did not answer.

McCoy entered the cell and was about to speak when Kirk held up a hand. T'Prylla pulled the boy forward and grasped him just under his left ear. "Grake was to have administered *ka nifoor* to his son when he turned twelve," T'Prylla said in Federation English. "He could not. Now he is not here, nor is Spock, so I must do it myself. That is irregular, but not unheard of." She had not taken her eyes from Radak's face.

"*Pstha na sochya olojhica, sfisth inoor Gracka?*" she asked. "Are you not blood of my blood, searching for the peace of maturity?"

Radak tried to turn his head away, but she grabbed his chin with her other hand and held him steady. Otherwise, he did not resist.

"Ages past, Vulcans bore the mark of heat, the scar of blowing sand and burning sun. The ground opened to eat us, the wind danced on our crops and leveled our cities. We wept for the pain, and we fought—"

Quick as a snake, Mason struck T'Kosa between her shoulders with knurled knuckles, instructed by the Spock within. T'Kosa went down as hard as the planetoid's light gravity allowed. Mason spun on the balls of her feet and administered a similar blow to T'Raus, who was not much better prepared to receive it. Then, she bent over the prone girl and placed her hand under her left ear. T'Raus was aware, but paralyzed temporarily. Mason suddenly found herself speaking Vulcan:

"Pstha na sochya olojhica, sfisth noor numkwa Gracka?" She listened to herself, fascinated. T'Raus's eyes widened. Mason wondered if the girl would suddenly just disappear. In the corridor ahead, there was the sound of scuffling. "None of your blood may administer, but are you not ready for the peace of maturity?"

—The question, Spock explained, may not be ignored by any Vulcan who knows how to speak our language. It is the signal for the activation of years of prior training, begun just after birth.

Mason began to intone more Vulcan words. "Ages past, Vulcans bore the mark of heat, the scar of blowing sand and burning sun. The ground opened to eat us—"

It took less than a minute. Radak's resistance seemed to melt as his mother progressed through the ritual. For a moment, Kirk thought the boy was going to cry—or scream with anguish—but T'Prylla continued, invoking all the ingrained responses subtly built in by Vulcan upbringing, eliminating—with the tacit consent of the child—the last vestiges of childish attitudes.

When she was done, she released Radak. The boy took a step backward, faltering, then sat down in his chair and rubbed his temples. "All that allowed Corona to move into you with such ease—all that is now gone," T'Prylla said. "There is very little time. What is it Corona plans to do, and how can we stop it?"

Kirk motioned for McCoy to turn on the translator recorder. Radak's eyes were the eyes of a very young Vulcan now, but with something more in them—the experience of ten years of Corona's presence. He seemed confused for a moment, but as T'Prylla sat across from him, he stammered and began to speak. He used Vulcan, but not a child's Vulcan. Kirk thought he sounded very much like Spock, though he hesitated now and then and scowled at the difficulty of expressing some of the concepts.

"Corona's universe was at nearly perfect thermal equilibrium," Radak began "and in that respect, it was very similar to the interior of a star. All was light and energy, extremely dense, and time was not as we know it today. Corona has a way to make this galaxy, at least—and perhaps the universe itself—as it was in the past, by altering local geometry. He wishes to shrink all matter down to where it will return to energy, and to re-create the monobloc— the fireball at the beginning. Then his kind can arise again, and the universe will become a place of life and activity, rather than the empty deadness of cold matter and stretched radiation."

"What's he talking about?" McCoy asked softly.

It took a moment for the meaning to sink in to Kirk. "He's describing the creation," Kirk said. "Corona wants to make our universe like it was in the first few minutes of creation."

"But what's he mean by 'empty deadness?' "

Radak heard and turned to McCoy and Kirk. "In the first three minutes of creation, there were more events, more complexity, than in the entire fifteen billion years since. Corona was a being of those times, and to its kind, the first three minutes seemed like an eternity. But the eternity came to an end, and they had to struggle to survive. The fireball cooled as it expanded, particles began to form into atoms, and all of Corona's kind perished. Only Corona remained, for it had discovered a way to 'echo' itself into existence wherever conditions were favorable. For the first few billion years after creation, Corona was able to appear frequently. The average temperature of the universe was much hotter than now, and the galaxies were forming. He was able to perform many experiments, some taking millions of years, and not succeeding.

"When the galaxies had formed and the universe

154

had cooled, Corona appeared much less frequently. Where mass anomalies in subspace disturbed the formations of young stars, it could resume its experiments. But only when it located our station did it find a way to work reliably with matter itself. Through us, it built machines to alter the structure of space-time, to expand the qualities of the very small into the very large."

"What will happen to us if he succeeds?" McCoy asked.

T'Prylla answered. "We are products of the 'dead' universe. We are like germs in a corpse. If the corpse comes back to life, the germs will be destroyed. We cannot survive in the world of Corona. The experiments which failed in the distant past—and which Corona tracked down with the Eye-to-Stars—involved the destruction of entire young galaxies. The results are quite familiar to us, though still mysterious.

"We call them quasars."

Mason wasn't sure what she had done, but she sat on an unresisting T'Raus. T'Kosa stood to one side like a mannequin. The sounds of struggle between Spock, Anauk and Grake had stopped. She got to her feet, uncertain what to do next.

—The ritual is finished. Now T'Raus must choose . . . Corona cannot impose its will on her.

Spock himself came down the corridor toward them. His face was bruised, and there was a cut over his right eye, but otherwise he was unhurt. As soon as she saw him, the Spock within her melted away like a flake of snow landing on a fingertip.

"You have administered *ka nifoor*?" he asked, bending over T'Raus.

"You have," she said. Spock touched the young female's face and she turned toward him.

"Is Corona within you?" Spock asked. The girl shook her head.

"It was a bad thing," she said. "It trapped mother

155

and father." She touched Spock's hand and Spock nodded his understanding.

"T'Raus is once again a young Vulcan," he said to Mason. "She does not have the experience, though she is mature. Corona must have concentrated on Radak, working first through him, then through his sister, then through his parents and Anauk and T'Kosa." He helped T'Raus to her feet. "Captain Kirk will have to make a decision. We must communicate with him soon, or we may not survive."

Mason felt a calm numbness. "Why?" she asked. "Corona isn't in charge now—" And suddenly she knew why. The "stolen" part of Corona was still inside her, and what it wanted to do became clear almost as soon as she asked. She didn't know whether to be awed or horrified.

"The process has already begun," Spock said. "The machinery in the research dome will soon begin altering the local structure of our universe. We must find a way to stop it, and to communicate with the *Enterprise*, before Kirk has to destroy the machinery, the station, perhaps the entire planetoid."

Chapter Twenty

Kirk sat in his chair on the bridge and ordered Sulu to bring the *Enterprise* to a new heading. "Ready phasers, full power. Load photon torpedoes."

Uhura repeatedly tried to contact the station, but received no reply. Kirk looked at her hopefully, but she had to shake her head. Veblen and McCoy came onto the bridge and without a word Veblen sat at the computer station. He checked the monitors and found them vigilant; Kirk had already fed them Radak's information. McCoy stood near the railing, knowing better than to say anything; knowing the decision Kirk now had to make.

Kirk leaned forward in his chair, watching the displays on the forward screen. The planetoid rotated slowly beneath them, a dead gray stretch of agglomerated rock. "Full mag on the station," he said. The screen image shifted several times in rapid succession and the *Enterprise* sensors tracked the station on multiple frequencies, displaying visible light. The two domes—research and storage—

showed up clearly. He could even make out the wreckage of the *Galileo II* on the landing platform. "Mr. Veblen, are there bodies in the shuttlecraft?"

Veblen swiveled his chair to the science console and keyed certain questions to the computers interpreting sensor data. "No, sir," he said.

"How many people within the station?"

"We can't scan the station interior, sir. Too much interference."

"Any idea what's happening inside the research dome?" Kirk asked, knowing the question was futile.

"No, sir," Veblen replied.

Kirk tapped his fingers on the chair arm edge. "Lieutenant Uhura, maintain open channels on all frequencies Spock might use to contact us. Mr. Veblen, what can we do about Corona itself?"

Veblen pursed his lips and shook his head. "The only manifestation is the radiation field and its extension around the planetoid, Captain. We cannot hope to shield anywhere near the area required to cut off its contact with the station."

"How about photon torpedoes applied along the extension of the field?"

"They would have no effect, sir. Photon torpedoes are not destructive on the level of fraction spaces."

"Then what in hell can we do?"

Veblen did not answer; the question was obviously rhetorical. The monitors knew what had to be done, however.

Kirk resumed tapping his fingers. He could not believe Spock was dead; somehow, he still sensed the reassuring presence of the Vulcan. He was certain Spock was alive and doing everything he could from within the station. Corona simply wasn't allowing them to communicate.

Communication—that was what was needed, and not just between the *Enterprise* and the station.

They had to find some way to communicate again with Corona. "Release T'Prylla and Radak and

158

bring them to the bridge, Devereaux," Kirk said. "Under guard."

"Without the Ybakra shield, sir?"

"Without the shield."

The security guard, standing at his station to the right of the elevator door, nodded and left the bridge.

Corona felt blind and deaf. After contact with the material intelligences, and so many years spent in their scale of time, observing through their sense organs, it took a while for Corona to adjust. There were still machines whose functioning it could monitor; but it had not planned for the loss of its Vulcan extensions, and so it could not immediately change what the machines were already doing.

This did not disturb Corona. The machines were working smoothly, expanding the foamlike space of the extreme basement of this dead universe. Corona felt as if it existed among the bones of its old universe, seeing hints of the distant past, but little more. It would be glad to have all things collapse through the expanded wormholes and singularities the machines would soon create; there would be a kind of joy in witnessing the sudden shrinking of the galaxy, from the viewpoint of Corona's fraction-space consciousness. And if the machines did succeed in creating a self-replicating singularity, weaving through all dimensions and subdimensions, Corona would gladly accept its own destruction. There would always be the final satisfaction of knowing that the universe had been rejuvenated.

And yet . . . there was a touch of regret. Strange as they were, the material intelligences had been quite interesting. Corona had never expected to find such complex beings in the bones of the old universe. If it was impossible to regard them with the same respect and affection Corona would have felt for its own kind, at least it acknowledged their usefulness. And they had shown remarkable flexibility in fighting back, ultimately wresting themselves from its control. That, too, was interesting.

But they would not survive if Corona succeeded. Nothing remotely like them would survive.

Tentatively, almost nostalgically, Corona extended tendrils of radiation to see if any of the Vulcans or the human had been made available to its touch again. And, somewhat to its surprise, it found Radak and T'Raus waiting.

It sensed a trap, but could not conceive of any way the material intelligences could harm it. They only had minutes, on their time scale, to prevent the machinery from completing its work.

"Corona is here," Radak announced. The boy looked to T'Prylla for guidance.

"Allow it in, give it a voice, but do not let it control you. You can resist it now."

"—Welcome," Radak said.

Corona did not reply, staring through the boy's eyes at the bridge of the *Enterprise*, at the human called Kirk and his companions. Simultaneously, on the planetoid, it touched T'Raus. She could not be controlled, either. To Corona, then, conversation was merely a matter of amusement until the final transform began.

"Mother," Radak said. "I can feel T'Raus. Corona links us."

"Who's with them?" Kirk asked.

"Our colleagues, your science officer and the human woman Mason."

"I need to speak with Corona," Kirk said. "And to know what is happening on the planetoid."

Radak reached out to touch T'Prylla. T'Prylla felt Corona's presence again, and steeled herself for the flood of undesired emotions—fear, resentment, hatred—but they did not come. Corona was undemanding, relaxed. Then, through Corona, she joined with T'Raus and saw through her eyes. "I am T'Raus," T'Prylla said.

"Spock!" Kirk demanded. "I need to speak with my science officer. Corona must stop the interference with our communications."

Radak spoke slowly and precisely—the voice of Corona. "I no longer interfere with your communications. There is disruption at the smallest levels of space-time between your ship and the planetoid. This I cannot stop."

In the background, Veblen checked the ship's most sensitive scientific equipment and ran diagnostics that could tell him more. He was particularly interested in certain peculiarities in the spectrum of excited hydrogen atoms; such a test was part of the warp drive diagnostics built into the ship's engines.

"Spock wishes to speak," T'Raus/T'Prylla said. "He will also accept Corona's touch now." T'Prylla's voice altered. "Captain, Spock here. Corona has succeeded. We cannot communicate because the machinery in the research dome has already begun altering the local continuum."

"Confirmed, Captain," Veblen said. "Ship's instrumentation is being affected."

"We must convince Corona of our worth," Spock said. "We have only minutes to spare, and there is nothing I can do here to stop the process."

A bright red light flashed on Kirk's command console—the monitors' warning signal. "What's that, Mr. Veblen?"

"The monitors are about to take over, Captain. You haven't acted quickly enough to destroy the station."

"Hold them off, Mr. Veblen!" He turned to Radak. "Corona! You must listen to me. We have the means to destroy everything you've tried to accomplish here. I won't be able to hold back the destruction for long. We must . . . come to an understanding. If we don't . . ." His face was anguished. "Good people will die. Friends, fellow workers, brilliant scientists. Do you know the meaning of friends?"

"All of my . . . friends . . . are eons dead," Corona/Radak said. "The universe is dead, and I will bring it back to life."

"No!" Kirk said. "The universe is *not* dead. We are here . . . and millions of other types of beings, occupying planets around the stars of this galaxy, and presumably all the other galaxies. There are even beings like yourself, not made of matter— beings like gods in comparison to Vulcans and humans. We have seen so little of what you call this dead universe, but we have seen enough to know . . . it is filled with life! With thought, and action, and hope . . . with the potential to grow, and develop. Your time is past . . . but ours has just barely begun. To try and bring back the past—"

"Captain!" Veblen cried out. The red light on Kirk's command console glowed steadily. "The monitors—"

Had taken over. "Mr. Sulu, bring the ship into firing position," their distinctive voice ordered. Sulu glanced at his captain, and in that moment of hesitation, the monitors assumed control of his post and the weapons console.

"No!" Kirk shouted, standing before his chair, holding out his arms.

The weapons console beeped, and below the bridge, the distant, shuddering bellow of emptying photon torpedo bays announced the *Enterprise*'s final course of action.

The torpedoes rushed toward the planetoid, their casings already dissolving in a fiery plasma of heavy bosons. Corona regarded them with interest; they tended to mimic the plasmas of the monobloc, though in a very crude way. A few seconds later, and Corona wouldn't have bothered with them, but they would impact before the machinery in the station was finished. Corona reached out and touched the torpedoes; they were not unlike the toys of its infancy, and there was a simple trick that could be worked on them. Corona disrupted their local parity. The torpedoes struck the planetoid and began their work of tearing it apart from a subatomic level. Then, abruptly, all the residual energy in the torpedoes was poured into a time-reversal. What little destruction they had accomplished was meticulously stitched back together in millionths of a second. The casings reformed and flew back toward the *Enterprise*, empty and harmless. The *Enterprise*'s shields rejected them and sent them gliding off into space.

For Corona, that had been amusing. But the infantile magic had disrupted the delicate machinery within the research dome, which was now automatically resetting itself before picking up where it had left off.

On board the *Enterprise*, the monitors ordered the ship to fire its phasers at the station, and maneuver for more photon torpedoes. Kirk sat helpless in his chair, and Veblen looked on with a fascinated kind of horror as the sensors once again showed a rapid decay in local reality.

Chapter Twenty-one

For Mason the sense of urgency was reduced by a kind of calm. She had little idea of what was actually happening. The Vulcans around her seemed to be steeling themselves for some cataclysm. Even Spock stood tall, hands folded behind his back, lips set grimly. There was nothing anybody could do; Corona was going to destroy them all. And why? As near as Mason could figure out, searching through the fragments of its memory within her, because Corona felt they were all bits of flotsam in a dead universe. Corona did not grasp what the new universe was really like. Mason stared from face to face for seconds, then walked across to the control platform where T'Raus and T'Kosa stood. She kept her eyes away from the demonstration sphere, which was filled with nonsense even more disturbing than what they had been subjected to before.

I am a writer, she thought. *It's my job to communicate. As often as not, I simply act as a chaperone for the recorders, jockeying them here and there so they can record everything. Then I sit down and edit and maybe try to make some sense out of it; not always, the machines are pretty good at that, too. But now and then, even on Yalbo, I get a chance to write—to communicate. God knows I'm not much of a talent, and I have all sorts of parochial views—hell, I'm bigoted—but . . .*

Sometimes, I know it, I can feel it—I can communicate. I can put my views across, perhaps better than anybody else. I can explain things. And I think I'd better start explaining, right now—nobody else seems to be getting the job done.

She reached inward, probing deeper into Corona's memories, and recoiled at their alienness. With an effort, she put away her revulsion and removed the last barriers separating Corona's memories and her own.

She looked up into T'Raus's eyes, now turned toward her, conveying her image to Corona.

"It's obvious you don't understand," Mason said. "If all these brilliant people can't explain it to you, I don't know how I will. But I hope you listen, anyway. I hope there's time.

"You see, we're all very young. Not nearly as old as you. And our world is very different." She mounted the platform and reached out for T'Raus's face, clenching her jaw hard and laying the tips of her fingers under T'Raus's temple. T'Raus reciprocated, and Mason was able to pass what she was thinking directly to Corona.

When Corona's memories mixed with her own, a specific image was cast up from her childhood—Yalbo's great billowing orange clouds, filled with nitric acid, deadly to breathe, absolutely marvelous to watch at sunset. From the broad viewports of the school, or the smaller windows of her home module, she had thought Yalbo's sky the most beautiful in the entire universe, with its oranges and greens and reds and yellows and warm mud colors. In the clouds she had built great floating palaces, magnificent curving highways; she had imagined creatures of all shapes

165

and sizes. When the wind blew the clouds along so briskly they crossed the sky from horizon to horizon in seconds, she could not imagine anything more lovely and free.

And then she had found tapes of Earth in the school library, and played them back.

"It was a shock," she said. "The skies of Earth seemed even more beautiful. You didn't need a suit to stand out under them. You could walk up mountains and touch clouds—or let them touch you. Right on your skin."

She felt Corona shudder at the thought of a constraining skin. She reached for an analogy, and found one. "Skin is like an event horizon in your world," she said. "In the earliest times, your people had to wait for the universe to grow broad enough that you could communicate with each other directly. You were all in little bubbles of space-time, unable to reach out. There was always Ybakra—you could talk, but you couldn't be with each other. Our skin sort of does that. We have to touch, talk, communicate so many ways because we cannot cross the barrier of our skins."

"Tell me more about clouds," T'Raus/Corona instructed.

Mason expanded on the topic. The clouds of matter in the early universe—created thousands of years after Corona's kind had died—had drifted in expanding space-time, slowly starting to clump and separate. "Then they lost their character, gave it up," she said, "to let other kinds of existence begin." That seemed confused, but she let it stand. "What would become clusters of galaxies formed out of the clouds, and then galaxies themselves. At first the galaxies were huge fuzzy spheres, but as they grew older, they flattened out. Then stars condensed from the clouds of gas in the young galaxies—"

I destroyed many of those young galaxies, Corona confided. *My failed experiments.*

Mason tried not to appear non-plussed. "Don't you see? They all had to share. Now, I can't be sure, but don't you suppose it's possible that the first clouds of matter were once capable of thought—and the clusters of galaxies, and the galaxies themselves? But as things changed, they died—they had to make way for new forms—"

Corona reacted in a way she could only describe as skeptical.

"Suppose they did," Mason continued. She was getting in way over her head. "And suppose that at some point, a galaxy rebelled—refused to change. And discovered that by doing so, it was dooming millions of new, smaller forms of intelligence to extinction. Wouldn't it be a . . ."

She had difficulty finding another analogy; she kept wondering how many seconds until they were all dead. She frowned in concentration. What was there in Corona's experience that could compare with what Corona was about to do now . . . "In your time, certain of your fellows refused to expand beyond their youthful event horizons. They wrapped themselves in very tight bubbles of space-time, because they were afraid of change. At first, they were tolerated, but as more and more individual realms joined, and as the universe grew larger, these hold-outs became dangerous. They could actually destroy others. They were murderers, not out of viciousness, but because they refused to change. Eventually they had to be hunted down and destroyed, in order to allow others to live. That's what the *Enterprise* is doing now—protecting itself against you."

She had kept her eyes closed as she spoke and thought all these things, but now she opened them. T'Raus was still regarding her steadily. "We all have to change," Mason said. "We all have to die, to make way for the new. If we try to live forever, we get in somebody's way, we stop something from

167

happening . . . someone from being born . . . and who knows, maybe the new will be an improvement on the old. Does that make sense?''

T'Raus did not convey an answer. She lifted her hand away from Mason's face, and Mason backed off a step, biting her lower lip. She felt very strange, all her thoughts caught somewhere between Corona's "memories" in her brain and her own childhood ruminations about clouds. "I'm sorry," she said, holding back a sensation of horror and sudden panic, believing she had wasted their last chance, when somebody else—perhaps Spock—could have been more effective. "I'm sorry!"

Despite the usefulness of the material intelligences, Corona had been convinced they were little more than peculiarities of the universe's decline. After all, they contributed nothing overall to the local universe but entropy; that is, they used energy but did not reduce the tendency to disorder which so characterized a dead continuum. In Corona's time, entropy had been the rule also, but the decline had barely been noticeable; the second law of thermodynamics had seemed a distant and unimportant possibility.

To Corona's way of thinking, the only significant intelligence would be one which at least hoped to rejuvenate its world . . .

Through T'Raus, Corona had listened to the human woman. Her words and thoughts served to occupy the long minutes before the continuum altered. But they did more than that. Particularly effective was her concern with "clouds," which suggested (again, crudely) the beauties of Corona's time, when solid things had been impossible, and all was beautiful flux. Among the Vulcans, Corona had never encountered the concept of "freedom"; the Vulcans were more concerned with adhering to a rigid code and following strict principles of logic, which rather puzzled Corona. So now it contemplated "freedom" as applied to the random motions of "clouds" and the behavior of material intelligences.

Freedom to move, to think, to accomplish; freedom to follow the dictates of one's needs. To exist.

Freedom was a very tricky concept. Too much could result in imposition on the freedom of another being; freedom could be contradictory. When the human woman pointed out that Corona was imposing on her own kind—and on many other material life-forms—by trying to end local reality, the image in her mind had been of clouds blown apart by a harsh, hot wind . . .

And that was something with which Corona could empathize. Thousands of years after the last generations of his kind, during his first reappearance, the universe had suddenly become transparent to the irritating little wavicles known as photons, light; instead of being bounced from particle to particle, the photons had streamed through the universe, conveying energy from place to place, blowing like a hot wind through the spaces that had once contained free and intelligent beings. The photon wind had dispersed the final remnants of Corona's kind.

By today's measure of time, the existence of Corona's people—their "eternity"—had spanned only a few minutes. They had survived many changes, but their end had finally come. Only Corona had found the means to travel the seemingly endless reaches of time, reappearing under certain conditions to reconstruct its Ybakra field.

These material beings knew what freedom was, then. And responsible freedom—as Corona construed it—meant a fight against entropy.

The phaser blasts had no effect, and all further torpedoes simply ceased to function, dissipating harmlessly against the planetoid. On the bridge of the *Enterprise*, the air seemed misty and electronic controls no longer functioned reliably. The ship's

169

computers, to Veblen's fascinated dismay, became little more than random number generators. The monitors struggled valiantly to maintain their control, but could not. They relied more on quantum subtleties than organic minds did; consequently, while the crew continued to function with only minor effects (so far), the monitors had no choice but to shut themselves down. It made little difference.

Kirk felt giddy. The sensation was not unlike the rush of exhilaration he felt when first entering warp drive—but tinged with a numbing sense of failure. The bridge seemed to be underwater; everything rippled in a way that was both nauseating and entrancing.

Veblen passed on his interpretations of data from the few instruments still functioning, those diagnostics built to survive warp engine stresses. Kirk listened as closely as he could; he was thinking of what he had seen in the demonstration sphere, when Corona had first tipped its "hand" about what it was up to. Would everything dissolve into the hypnotic chaos of the very small? Where would the *Enterprise* be in such a maelstrom? Where would Kirk be?

McCoy had never been more terrified. If everything came unwound, he was convinced he knew what lay on the other side—and that was nothing less than Hell. No ministrations possible, no healing, only endless lack of control, giving in to the tortures imposed by those inner forces which he could not face. "I pity poor Spock," he thought, feeling a rush of cameraderie for the Vulcan he had pestered so mercilessly over the years . . . and had felt so much respect for.

Spock, however, still stood in a sea of comparative calm. The machines in the research dome had created a tiny, unaffected bubble about themselves to keep working properly until they had finished their task. Spock had listened to Mason's words, had picked up on some of the thoughts passed through Corona, and had been puzzled and intrigued by this

170

extraordinary and irrational approach. Pleading a case was alien to all of Vulcan culture; either a thing was, or it was not. Persuasion and opinion had little role in Vulcan life.

Grake, T'Kosa, Anauk, Spock—and on the *Enterprise* T'Prylla—all had made their final peace with existence.

Chapter Twenty-two

From horizon to horizon, the sky was filled with a dark purple glow, broken by wisps of milky white and luminous green. Mason felt the crunch of ages-old pebbles beneath her shoes, the only sound besides her breathing. The new suns were coming into view beyond the irregular edge of the planetoid, swathed in the dusty, gassy yoke of their recent birth.

She reached out her hand, uncertain why she was here, or how she was surviving. The faint greenish iridescence of the envelope surrounding her, flashed briefly as if in answer to one question, and then, overhead, the Eye-to-Stars unfolded and threw a brilliant spotlight beam on her. She looked up and shielded her eyes with her hand.

"Behind you, please," a voice said. She turned and jumped back in surprise. An indistinct orange cloud was in the envelope with her, roiling and spreading under the influence of unfelt winds. "This is a shape you have taught me, which I find very pleasing. I am what T'Prylla calls Corona."

Mason didn't know what to say, so she said nothing.

"Where are you from?"

She stammered, caught herself, and tried to answer smoothly. "From a planet called Yalbo." This is a dream, she thought. I'm almost dead and I'm dreaming.

"It must be a very beautiful place," Corona said. "Is it?"

"That you see so much beauty in it. That formations in its . . . atmosphere can convey the notion of freedom to you, and through you, to me." The cloud darkened as if passing beyond sunset. "Or perhaps it is that you are beautiful, to find such beauty wherever you may be."

"I'm . . . I'm very frightened," Mason said. "You are the strangest thing—being—I've ever known."

"And yet, you have some of my memories within you, conveyed by the Vulcan-human Spock. Your kind is strange to me, as well. Perhaps we can overcome our unfamiliarity if we exchange."

"Exchange?"

"There has been much teaching in the past few . . . hours . . . but not nearly enough. I have an imperfect understanding of your mode of being, your human kind. Even after ten years, it is now apparent I understand little about your fellows, the Vulcans. I request an exchange of experiences. I will complete the memories within you, as much as you wish to have, and you will share your experiences with me. I will take them with me . . . to the region you see now, in the Eye-to-Stars."

"Where is that? A new stellar system?"

There was silence for a moment. "It does not exist in your here-now. It is a distant possibility. Much time must pass. All the stars and galaxies will grow old and fade, the universe will be filled with black holes, the black holes will return their mass to the emptiness and become naked singularities. Time itself will grow old, come to a stop. What happens

173

after is difficult to understand—emptiness, even more desolation than now."

"That doesn't look very empty," Mason said, shielding her eyes.

"You have given me a notion of alternatives . . . other means of achieving my goal than destroying this universe. What the Eye-to-Stars shows is an alternative, if I survive beyond the emptiness and darkness. When all else has come to a stop, and the universe seems completely dead, I will be a focus. There will be nothing but the radiation of fraction spaces—what you call Ybakra. I will channel that radiation and fill the void once again. There will be no need for machinery, matter, anything extra . . . only myself."

She had a wild hope that perhaps she *wasn't* dreaming.

"Is this what you wished?" Corona asked. "That your reality be spared, so that you might all pursue a course to freedom?"

"Are we being spared?" she asked.

"Yes. The machines are reversing themselves now. I have returned the others in the station to the *Enterprise*, all but the frozen ones. I await instructions on their disposition."

Of all the things to occur to her next, Mason had to resort to her reporter's suspicious nature and ask, "But I thought you couldn't transform anything much larger than a child."

"While the machinery was absorbing so much energy, no," Corona said.

"Why did you stop your machines?"

"Because you made me aware that in ages to come, we may share the same goal. Perhaps your kind will succeed in controlling entropy," Corona said. "In which case, the universe will not die . . . at least not in the way that seems most likely. And I will not be needed. Still, you could fail. You are young—even those mentioned by the human Kirk, those who seem god-like to you. You have a long time in which to grow, and prepare yourselves, and you could make mistakes. You could fail. If you do not succeed, then perhaps I will."

"You mean, my descendants could save the universe?"

"Your kind. You are kin to all beings made of matter, or which arose from matter. In my eyes, you are all very much the same. Any differences are minor."

Mason stared straight into the middle of the cloud, so very like the clouds she had seen and wondered about as a child. So very like the clouds that had haunted her dreams. "Yes," she said, swallowing hard.

"You will trade full memories with me?"

She nodded. "As many as I can."

Chapter Twenty-three

"Dr. McCoy."

The voice interrupted his reverie. He had been contemplating death—more death than he had ever before conceived of, the death perhaps of everything —on the bridge of the *Enterprise*. There had been a moment of disorientation, an unpleasant sensation of travel, and now—

He saw T'Kosa standing before him. "What in the name of—"

"Mason tells us you are the one to speak to."

McCoy glanced around. They stood outside the cold storage cylinder on the station. His amazement would have been comical to a human, but not to the Vulcan female. "About what?"

"Where the sleepers should be transformed."

"I . . . I don't understand."

"There is not much time. Corona's remaining time here is less than three minutes. The shuttle is destroyed, and the personnel cannot be quickly brought up to the ship by transporter. Only Corona can move them now." T'Kosa watched him closely, obviously interested in his reaction-time and flexibility. And McCoy—whatever the situation—was not about to let her find him inadequate.

"Of course," he said, pulling himself together. "Space has been cleared in the sickbay, battle casualties section. Each hibernaculum has a power hookup, and the . . . transform will have to be smooth enough so that there's no fluctuation in their temperature."

"Very well," T'Kosa said. "We will accompany them."

"No—wait!"

But it was too late. As far as McCoy was concerned, transforming was far worse than transporting. This time, he was fully aware every step of the way.

Chapel stood at one end of the battle casualty ward, mouth open. The medical slate dropped from her hand as, one by one, thirty hibernacula appeared in their assigned positions. Energy conduits whined at the increased power load. The sickbay lights dimmed briefly, then returned to normal.

In security, Olaus registered an invasion of the *Enterprise*'s hull by an extraordinary amount of mass—at least thirty metric tons.

In engineering, the assistant watch officer made note of an extra power load.

On the bridge, McCoy reappeared in his accustomed position behind the railing. Uhura witnessed his materialization, but was too stunned by the chain of events in the past few minutes to react. Then, beside him, Spock and four other Vulcans materialized, just as Kirk swiveled in the captain's chair.

"Bones—"

"Don't ask," McCoy said. "There isn't time. I have to get down to sickbay." He entered the elevator.

"Spock?"

"I am completely unaware of what has happened, Captain. Where is Mason?"

Kirk gaped. "How the hell should I know? And what in God's name is going on?"

Veblen finished his sensor sweep and turned to Kirk. "Captain, the local continuum has returned to normal. Ship's instruments are functioning properly."

"We're not dead," Sulu said, and that seemed to sum it all up very well.

All eyes were on Kirk when Mason materialized next to his chair. They stared at each other and Mason smiled—almost smugly.

"Corona suggests the *Enterprise* retreat to a distance of at least a billion kilometers," she said crisply. "Corona's presence in this nebula is waning, and it can no longer vouch for the stability of the machines in the research station."

"Helmsman—" Kirk began.

"Course laid in," Sulu said. "Executing." The *Enterprise*'s impulse engines cut in and vibrated every deck in the saucer with their sudden burst of power. The ship spiraled away from the planetoid, flattening the orbital curve to very nearly a straight line as Kirk ordered maximum acceleration.

Mason continued to stand near the captain's chair, but she was hardly aware of the activity. She was receiving the last of Corona's Ybakra signals.

Deep below the measures of status geometry, the subspace mass anomalies were separating and breaking up on several geodesics impossible for the human mind to visualize. The conditions which had allowed Corona to manifest in the nebula were now ending—perhaps not to be duplicated for billions of years. And Mason knew that even if the conditions did arise again, Corona would not return. Only at the very last—if all else failed, if all their descendants in the new universe of emptiness and free-traveling photons and matter could not halt entropy's triumph

—only when there was nothingness and death and no freedom—

Only then would Corona return, to fulfill a promise made at the beginning of time.

One more favor, she asked.

What might that be? came the weakening response.

There is still a minor problem . . . And she specified the problem. *Can you solve it?*

The reply was almost too weak to make out, but she thought it was an affirmative. Then she said, "Good-bye," but no reply came. The contact had already been severed.

Spock stood next to Veblen, watching the sensors as the *Enterprise* sped away. "Captain, the planetoid is breaking up," he said. He switched on computer graphics to interpret what then occurred.

Mason watched the forward screen, feeling Corona's past within her, almost as real as her own. On a small scale, the screen showed what Corona had planned for an incomprehensibly larger region of space-time.

The planetoid slowly and smoothly turned inside out, revealing all of its amorphous interior as if through a distorting lens. Behind it, two elongated darknesses yawned, drawing the planetoid out into an ellipse, then a cylinder, flaring the ends, swallowing them . . . and stretching what remained into a fine thread, which vanished below the limits of resolution. For a half million kilometers around, the nebula's gases were sucked into the space-time chasm.

At the center of the invisible thread, a tiny and incomplete new universe blossomed. At first it was only a few centimeters in diameter, releasing very little light and appearing dull brown in color. Then, as all the matter within the half-million kilometer slice of the nebula rushed back into normal space, transformed into pure energy, the orb expanded and turned a mottled, brilliant orange. The orange became green, and the green became a blue so intense the sensors shut themselves down. The forward screen went black.

The brilliance faded quickly. The new universe was not stable, and all the potential within it could not compete with the established stresses of status geometry. Its energy was squandered. All that remained was a tiny sun, joining its slightly older companions, a weak and inconstant sibling.

It did not last long. By the time the *Enterprise* had reached its position of safety, the glow had vanished completely, and there was nothing to distinguish the Black Box Nebula from any of the other emission nebulas dotting the spiral arms of the Galaxy.

Chapter Twenty-four

McCoy wasted no time thinking about what had just happened to him. He walked through the battle casualties section of the sickbay, medical tricorder in hand. The hibernacula were in place and the sleepers had not been damaged any further. Theoretically, their reconstruction could begin at any time. And yet after all that had happened, the medical monitors still blocked the way.

Chapel stood beside him when he was finished. "Mr. Spock is waiting in the computer control center," she said.

"I'm tired," he said abruptly, closing his eyes. "Is this any time to ask me to argue with a bunch of computerized ghosts?"

Chapel tried to appear sympathetic. "Mr. Spock—"

"Yes, yes, I know," McCoy grumbled. "Time's awastin'." He stood for a moment longer, his muscles aching with tension, peering down the two rows of hibernacula. "God knows why *any* of us is still alive."

In the computer control center, Spock waited by the monitors' console. Veblen sat nearby, hands folded tightly in his lap. Only because of Spock's assurances that they were not about to do anything illegal had Veblen given them access. Even so, the unorthodox approach bothered him. Like McCoy, the stress of the past few hours pierced his stomach and muscles like dull leaden needles.

The last thing he wanted was a fight over the monitors. He had come to hate them, both for their inadequacies and for the duties they forced upon him. Still, he would not relent.

McCoy sat down at the console. Spock called up the first of the experience memories within the medical monitors, and arranged for vocal communication. "Whom am I talking to?" McCoy asked him. "And is he or she alive or dead?"

"Dead now, I believe," Spock said. "You will speak to the memories of Commodore of the Medical Corps Elias R. Rostovtzev."

"Hell, Spock, he was my professor at Starfleet Medical Academy!"

"I realize that, Doctor. He is the only one you have had prior acquaintance with."

"He damned near flunked me."

Spock raised an eyebrow. "I can call up another experience memory if you wish."

"No, no . . . he'll do. How much of a personality is left in there, Spock?"

"Only patterns, Doctor. For this function, the monitors provide basic reasoning and question-and-answer abilities. The Commodore is not alive in the system, if that is what you are asking." Still, Spock had his doubts that was a completely accurate assessment. Admiral Harauk had been rather more active in the system than he had expected—active, and independent.

"Okay. I'm ready."

There was nothing for McCoy to look at—only the console display, blanked for vocal communication.

Carrier frequency hiss filled the speakers, and a sensation of someone waiting . . . a definite and very spooky presence.

"Commodore Rostovtzev?"

"Yes." The voice was tinny but recognizable. "Who's speaking?"

"McCoy, Doctor Rostovtzev. Leonard McCoy."

"Lieutenant JG Leonard McCoy?"

"Lieutenant Commander now, Doctor. Medical officer of the U.S.S. *Enterprise.*"

"Why haven't you made commander, Leonard? Been slacking again?"

McCoy flushed. "No, sir. I'm not quite sure where to begin . . ."

"At the beginning, Leonard," the voice said patiently.

"There's a decision you'll be called upon to make—" McCoy began. Veblen rose from his seat to protest—this was coming much too close to tampering with the monitors—but Spock stopped him. Veblen sat down reluctantly, poised to interrupt.

"Yes. There are six of us here, Leonard, if I remember correctly. Not that any of us are actually here, you understand."

"It's rather a fine distinction, sir."

"Be that as it may. Continue."

"You're to administer laws regarding the TEREC system aboard the *Enterprise*—"

"Ah, yes," Rostovtze said. "The thirty sleepers subjected to Ybakra. I believe this problem has been presented to us already."

"Yes, sir. I was hoping to discuss the case with you in more detail."

"Why? The monitors have given their go-ahead. We won't stand in the way of reconstruction."

McCoy's and Veblen's jaws dropped simultaneously. "But sir—"

"Get busy, man! I'm—we're—very interested in the procedures. Surely you're anxious to proceed."

"Yes, sir!" He stood, glanced at Veblen and Spock, and shrugged. "I'll get right on it."

Veblen sat at the console as soon as McCoy was out of the room. He checked all program codes and safeguards. None had been tampered with. The monitors were intact. "Mr. Spock, this is impossible . . ."

"Clearly not, Mr. Veblen. It has happened." Spock left the control center. Veblen ran his checks several more times, without finding any hint of why the ruling had changed.

On his last sweep, however, he played back the laws governing the use of the TEREC. He specifically called up the law regarding resuscitation of inanimate beings, and set his search for embedded definitions of "inanimate."

The definition ran on for several paragraphs of text. As he read through the paragraphs, he sensed a subtle shift in tone, nothing he could quite pin down . . . until he scanned the last line. His eyes widened. It read:

"There shall not be any attempt to stand in the way of that which could further the cause of life, freedom or the war against entropy, no matter what laws may read, or duty may require." This was followed by an equation which had no place in medical definitions. He puzzled out the equation for several minutes, and then realized what it was.

The equation precisely described certain active states of fraction space radiation—Ybakra, to be precise.

It was a signature.

Veblen began to laugh, and then to cry, and laugh again, burying his head in his arms on the console keyboard.

Chapter Twenty-five

The *Enterprise* began its return voyage, with two stops scheduled between the Black Box Nebula and Starbase 19.

First, they would return Mason to Yalbo. She was not particularly upset by the thought of becoming a small-planet girl once again. Because of what she now was—what she held within—wherever she spent her time would be an exotic place. Corona had provided her with an unfailing sense of the new and unexpected. The *Enterprise* would then make a long loop to the stellar system of Epsilon Eridani, where they would drop off the Vulcans of Station One on their home world.

Grake and T'Prylla received Spock in their quarters with old-family Vulcan ritual, offering him first a favorite aphorism engraved on an expended dilithium crystal, then a brief session of meditation, followed by a formal Vulcan supper. No apologies were offered for what had happened; obviously, none were necessary. They behaved as if the Black Box incident had been some far-off dramatic performance, fascinating and puzzling, but hardly worthy of recriminations. After the supper utensils had been cleansed by the entire group, Radak and T'Raus performed the honor of wiping their visitor's hands. T'Prylla then spoke. "Spock, there was mention of a change in the Science Academy. What sort of change?"

Spock returned his cleansed hands to the sleeves of his robe. "I believe there is interest in accepting your logical methods as alternative paths to the Way. Perhaps, in the past few days, we have seen the inadequacies of a too-rigid approach to the teachings of Surak. Only through the mind of a human did Corona begin to understand the inadvisability of its actions. How are we to understand this failure on our part?"

"If my alternatives had been of value, surely Corona would have realized error while occupying our minds. My family and colleagues are all well-versed in my methods."

"Then there is room for debate and progress all around." Spock bowed from his seated position as Anauk and T'Kosa entered.

"We have been aiding McCoy with the TEREC," T'Kosa said. "I must revise my estimates of human behavior. He seems to harbor no ill-will toward us."

"Humans, unlike Vulcans, are hardly predictable," Spock said. Among the Vulcans, this truism aroused the equivalent of a humored response; they lifted the last three fingers of their left hands in appreciation.

Mason revealed what she could about her role in the affair before Spock, Kirk and McCoy in a senior officer's closed-door meeting in Kirk's quarters. When Spock questioned her about Corona, she replied, quite truthfully, "I know very little about it . . . not much more than you left in my mind, Mr. Spock." But she was learning every day. "I do know that the medical monitors have been tampered with. I requested it, and I will take responsibility."

"You . . . requested it?" Kirk asked.

"Yes. If you military types can't get your act together, then it's up to us civilians to help you out." Kirk was about to protest when he saw the twinkle in her eye—and that now-common touch-of-smugness grin.

She did not reveal any more than she had to about Corona. That was a private thing, and if someday it had to be made public—as she acknowledged it almost certainly would—well, she would be better prepared, more mature. Less bigoted. Corona was her ticket to inner peace.

Spock—who probably knew there was much she wasn't saying—did not press her, and she was grateful.

The next morning, another meeting was held—more formal and more somber—in the main conference room.

"Gentlemen, this inquiry is hereby called to order. Captain James T. Kirk presiding." Kirk banged the ceremonial gavel, feeling slightly grand and very foolish as he always did in such circumstances. "Our duty is to judge the efficacy of the monitors aboard the *Enterprise*, especially in relation to our recent mission. Dr. McCoy, I believe you have an opening comment to make."

McCoy stood and glanced around the table at Kirk, Spock, Scott, Veblen, Olaus and Mason. Mason's replacement recorder floated near her shoulder. "I'm not much of a legal wizard," he admitted. "I don't know how we will overcome further difficulties with the medical monitors." He glanced at Mason, then at Veblen.

Veblen said nothing.

"I'm just grateful we've solved our present problems. The reconstruction is well under way, and in four days we'll have the first two healthy and in need of temporary living quarters. Mr. Veblen, however good an idea the medical monitors were in Federation chambers, out here, they don't work. The *Enterprise* was sent on this mission specifically because we had the new equipment, but our mission came very close to being hamstrung from the beginning. Too close. I dislike relying on miracles."

"Thank you, Dr. McCoy. Mr. Spock, your analysis of the monitors' role in the Corona incident?"

"Captain." Spock stood, looking at nobody in particular. "The command monitors backed up your decisions until the very last moment, when they decided you were not acting quickly enough to stop the threat. On examining the monitors' internal records, Mr. Veblen and I have found that all six of the experience-memories of Starfleet command-rank officers agreed unanimously that you did not act soon enough. Yet the outcome may not have been affected by the monitors' takeover—indicating your judgment may not have been faulty. Further analysis is necessary."

Spock sat down and Kirk nodded at Veblen. The computer officer stood, his eyes meeting Mason's on the other side of the table. "The monitors functioned exactly as intended. In that sense, they are successes. However . . ." He pulled a datapack from his belt. "I believe the monitors have some severe drawbacks, not the least of them being . . . they can be tampered with. That is, they can be affected by . . . quantum instabilities. The medical monitors have clearly been shown to be inadequate. I sympathize with Dr. McCoy's frustration. I believe we will have no difficulty convincing the Federation that certain strictures should be lifted, and certain advancements in medical science be taken into account." He glanced at Mason as if looking for an explanation. She returned his look with a pleasant smile.

"With regard to the command monitors . . . Personally, I believe Captain Kirk should not have been overridden, that he was conducting himself in the best manner possible, and that his action, or inaction, did not jeopardize the *Enterprise,* the mission or . . ." He had almost said "the universe," but that sounded comically grandiose. "Or anything else. I will recommend adjustments in the command monitors as well."

There was no further testimony. Kirk adjourned the meeting, and after the room was cleared, walked alone to his quarters. Halfway there, he was hailed by Mason. "May I speak with you, Captain?"

"Certainly."

She walked abreast of him, looking down at the deck. "What do you think of the monitors, Captain? Personally, I mean."

"Finishing your story?"

"I don't know," Mason said. "Perhaps. I don't feel much like a reporter now. I don't know what I am, exactly. I've . . . become very involved in the story. I'm no longer objective."

They arrived at the door to his quarters. "Personally, I'll tell you. But only off the record."

"All right."

"Off the record," he reiterated, "I think the monitors were correct. I have a hunch that firing at the station gave us a few extra seconds, maybe minutes. I don't know how, but that's what I feel. I hesitated, because I was concerned about Spock, the Vulcans, you . . . I was too concerned." He opened the door and stepped inside.

"Will you request that the monitors be removed?" Mason asked.

He shrugged. "You know, there's another aspect . . ."

"Still off the record?"

"Yes. If the monitors hadn't been there—if I hadn't sensed they would take over, and remove the responsibility from my shoulders—would I have fired on the station?"

"Would you have?"

"I don't know. It's a question I'll have to live with."

He shut the door and went to his desk to make an entry in his personal log, but it was several hours before he could bring himself to begin.

Mason joined Veblen in the officer's lounge. "Share a table with me?" Veblen asked. She agreed and they picked up their trays of food from the autochef.

"I suppose you know what the ship's scuttlebutt is," Veblen said. "Word's gotten around about your debriefing."

"I wasn't the only one. I wasn't even the only human. There was Chekov, Spock and the six Vulcans from the station."

"But you were the only one who could testify about Corona's motivation. That's the scuttlebutt, anyway. Is it true?"

She shook her head in dismay. "I'm supposed to be a reporter. I'm not supposed to be the center of a story."

Veblen urged her to continue. When she refused, he reminded her of an earlier conversation. "As one outcast to another," he said. "How do you know about Corona's motivations?"

"You're so very curious," Mason responded. Her grin was thoroughly wicked.

"I have my reasons," Veblen said. "I thought you might be able to clear up some mysteries."

"Why don't you ask Corona yourself? Through me, if you believe that's possible."

"You mean . . ."

"Eat your lunch. We've all got problems."

In the next sleep period, in Uhura's quarters, she listened to the communications officer singing old

190

African lullabies. There was a song about children harnessing the clouds of a very old mountain, and riding them from sleep to dawn.

Within Mason, there was a reaction not entirely her own . . . a feeling of the deepest pleasure, and nostalgia.

It did not alarm her. It was, in fact, something of a comfort.

"You know," she said when the song was over, "that Mr. Spock is quite a fellow . . ."

Uhura laughed and reached out for Mason's hand. "That a girl," she said, squeezing her fingers.

Captain's Log, Stardate 4997.54.

While I wrestle with some very troubling thoughts, I look back over what's happened . . . and a sensation of the deepest astonishment overcomes me.

My crew, myself—we're all fallible, capable of many different kinds of failure. The Vulcans are . . . I was about to say "only human," but I mean in the sense they, too, are limited. Now I look back over Mason's confidential testimony . . . and though I suspect she has hardly told us everything, I marvel.

What other group of human beings has ever experienced a life as broad, as surprising, as full as the crew of this ship? We have seen things, been places, accomplished missions almost beyond imagining . . . at least for a staid, romantic fellow like myself.

Sometimes, however, I think I would have been just as content to pilot some system craft between planets. At least then, I wouldn't have to live with this ache, this fear that I am not fitted for my task . . . that if I had been left to my own devices, perhaps the Galaxy . . . the universe! Dear God . . . would no longer exist. Can anyone face such a test, such a judgment?

What an incredibly strange universe this is, that a cry from its very infancy can echo across all eternity . . . and pose such challenges for me, for us all.